Samuel French Acting Edition

The Glitter Girls

by Mark Dunn

I0591789

‖SAMUEL FRENCH‖

SAMUELFRENCH.COM   SAMUELFRENCH.CO.UK

MUSIC USE NOTE

Licensees are solely responsible for obtaining formal written permission from copyright owners to use copyrighted music in the performance of this play and are strongly cautioned to do so. If no such permission is obtained by the licensee, then the licensee must use only original music that the licensee owns and controls. Licensees are solely responsible and liable for all music clearances and shall indemnify the copyright owners of the play(s) and their licensing agent, Samuel French, against any costs, expenses, losses and liabilities arising from the use of music by licensees. Please contact the appropriate music licensing authority in your territory for the rights to any incidental music.

IMPORTANT BILLING AND CREDIT REQUIREMENTS

If you have obtained performance rights to this title, please refer to your licensing agreement for important billing and credit requirements.

THE GLITTER GIRLS opened at the Village Playhouse in West Allis, Wisconsin on December 1, 2017. The director was Scott Sorensen. The producers were Laura LaPinske and Judy Lee Tarbox. The stage manager was Lynn Ruhl. The set designer was Scott Sorensen. Set artwork was by Veronica Shmauz. Costumes were by Rosie Peterson. The lighting design was by Elizabeth Havican. The props mistress was Kelly Taylor-Schaus. The program design was by Erico Ortiz. The cast, in order of appearance, was as follows:

ARPEGE LACROIX	Mark Gormican
TRUDY TROMAINE	Kathy Landry
PATTY WESLEY	Dana Vetter
CHARLIE SEABURN	Clayton Mortl
VALERIE FAIRHOPE	Sam Billeck
FLOSSIE PRICE	Donna McMaster
MAYVONNE RAUSCH	Rosie Peterson
MAMIE EWING	Anne Gorski
CORINNE CULVERT	Jackie Benka
DOWD FOSTER	Larry Rowe

CHARACTERS

in order of appearance

ARPEGE LACROIX A.K.A. ARNOLD CROSS – Of indeterminate age. Arpege, who is Trudy Tromaine's maid, was born Arnold Cross. He considers himself "as feminine as is required" (this requirement to be revealed in the script). Because Arpege is basically a slob he doesn't go to great lengths to convince others that he is a woman. A wig, a smear of lipstick, a dress, and high-heel shoes are representative of his best effort along these lines. Toward the end of the play he will revert to Arnold, his remaining lines of dialogue assigned to Arnold rather than to Arpege.

TRUDY TROMAINE – Sixty, rich as all-get-out (as they say in the South), and eccentric with a capital E. Trudy is president and founder of "The Glitter Girls," a woman's social club and, sometimes, charitable organization. Trudy understands that she has a town reputation for color and flamboyance and wears that reputation with pride.

PATTY WESLEY – Twenty-two, the youngest Glitter Girl, but quite comfortable in the company of her older G.G. sisters. Patty is a work-in-progress, smart and analytical, feisty but only occasionally confrontational. Patty is pursuing her master's degree in social work at a local university.

CHARLIE SEABURN – Twenty-two, son and "representative" of the absent Barbara Seaburn. Charlie is studying to become a lawyer like his mother. He defaults to bashfulness and is not nearly as assertive as he would like to be, the result, some would say, of having lived most of his life under the thumb of a domineering, single parent. But he's working hard to overcome his deficiencies.

VALERIE FAIRHOPE – Forty-five, a former exotic dancer whose face, though hardened and furrowed with the years, still maintains a youthful beauty and vibrancy. As a Zumba fitness instructor, Val also boasts a shapely figure she's not shy about showing off through the somewhat revealing clothing she wears. Val has been beaten up by life but has refused to stay down for the count.

FLOSSIE PRICE – Fifty-eight, grew up in rural poverty but won her personal sweepstakes when she was swept off her feet and put into both a dental chair and a wedding dress by a local dentist, the unfortunately named Vincent Price. Flossie has come far but maintains a hillbilly sensibility and manner of speaking.

MAYVONNE RAUSCH – At seventy-four the oldest Glitter Girl, but by no means the archetypal "little old lady." Mayvonne's disposition is sweet and mothering, but she won't be pushed around. Mayvonne was a junior high school teacher, long married but now widowed. It is very hard not to like this lovely, well-groomed, well-disposed, and very smart (though occasionally marmish) woman.

MAMIE EWING – Sixty-four, the wife of a town councilman (and soon-to-be candidate for mayor) and owner of her own dress shop; a handsome, exquisitely-dressed woman with a sophisticated air about her (or as close to sophistication as one gets in Hickman Hills). Mamie can't help it that she's abrasive and puts people off; it just comes naturally.

CORINNE CULVERT – A fairly attractive thirty-six, but going through one hell of a bad time right now, which shows in her bedraggled expression and in the laggard, plodding way she carries herself about. Corinne's husband is the bane of her existence, though she can't help loving him. A familiar trope.

DOWD FOSTER – Fifty-five, a recent widower. His late wife, Mary Katherine, was a Glitter Girl, and he has joined the others to honor her memory and to show respect for all of the women who had been her friends. Dowd is a good ol' boy if there ever was one. He has been a good provider and a loving father to his son and daughter. Dowd owns a tire store.

SETTING

The play takes place in the fictional North Georgia town of Hickman Hills in late May of this year. Hickman Hills is like most southern small towns: Mayberry on the outside, Peyton Place on the inside. It's the kind of American hamlet where people generally try to mind their own business...and generally fail. Over the last decade or so the town has seen a marked increase in commercial and residential development, as either welcoming recipient or victim (depending on how one feels about such a thing) of ineluctable Atlanta suburban sprawl.

Hickman Hills has watched its long-abandoned burlap factory turned into a successful concern for the weaving and marketing of fashionable woolen snoods*, eventually earning itself the proud moniker "Snood Capital of the World." This is no stray fact of local trivia. A sudden caprice on the part of the woman who almost single-handedly put the town on the international fashion map does, in fact, serve as chief catalyst for this play.

The Glitter Girls takes place on the back porch and adjoining backyard of one Trudy Tromaine, Hickman Hills' richest and most illustrious resident.

***snood** (snōōd) *n.* 1. an ornamental bag-like hat or hairnet generally worn at the back of a woman's head. 2. the fleshy appendage that hangs from a turkey's upper beak.

AUTHOR'S NOTES

How the Characters Voted

KEY (characters listed in order of appearance):

PW:	Patty Wesley
CS:	Charlie Seaburn
VF:	Valerie Fairhope
FP:	Flossie Price
MR:	Mayvonne Rausch
ME:	Mamie Ewing
CC:	Corinne Culvert
DF:	Dowd Foster

Character	Round One	Round Two	Round Three	Round Four
PW:	VF	VF	FP	FP
CS:	CC	CC	CC	FP
VF:	ME	MR	CC	FP
FP:	VF	PW	PW	PW
MR:	ME	MR	–	–
ME:	CC	–	–	–
CC:	ME	VF	VF	–
DF:	MR	MR	CC	FP

The Glitter Girls is dedicated to all those theatre folk in the United States and Canada who responded to my query about this brand-new play, who asked to see a script, who circulated the script among their boards and their directors, and who ultimately scheduled it for production, from the Village Playhouse in Wisconsin to the East Mountain Centre for Theatre in New Mexico, from the James Downey Theatre in Illinois to Playhouse 2000 in Texas and the Tupelo Community Theatre in Mississippi, and all the others. You are the reason I've enjoyed working in this odd profession for the last thirty years. So how about we do this for another thirty?

ACT ONE

Scene One

(Lights come up on Trudy Tromaine's back porch and adjoining back lawn and herb garden. This being the American South, the porch ought to be screened in, but since so much of the action of the play takes place here accommodations should be made for audience accessibility. The porch is decked out in matching white wicker furniture and potted plants.)

*(**ARPEGE LACROIX** steps out onto the porch from inside the house. He is dressed casually [perhaps a tied-off blouse and capri pants] and carries a tray containing a pitcher and several glasses. He sets it on a wicker roll-cart. He goes to a table and tidies up a spread of assorted fruit slices and finger foods. A moment later he is joined by **TRUDY TROMAINE**, who also emerges from the house. She's carrying several throw pillows. These she distributes thoughtfully among the various chairs and loveseats. She steps back and gives the porch a good looking-over.)*

TRUDY. *(To **ARPEGE**.)* Okay. What else?

ARPEGE. *(Also studying the porch arrangement.)* Looks fine to me.

TRUDY. And how do *I* look?

ARPEGE. Lovely as always.

TRUDY. That was sweet, but I'm supposed to be dying.

ARPEGE. Who says a dying woman can't be beautiful?

TRUDY. The point, Arpege, is that I have to be convincing. I have weeks – possibly only days – to live. Death is clawing at my door.

ARPEGE. *(After thinking this over for a moment.)* Maybe if you sucked in your cheeks a little more.

> *(Which he does to show how this would look.)*

Okay. Now squeeze your eyes and make a mouth that looks like it's covered in painful cold sores. See?

> (**ARPEGE** *shows* **TRUDY** *how this would look as well.)*

TRUDY. You look constipated.

ARPEGE. Excuse me for living, but I'm trying to help.

TRUDY. Tell me if these smudges I put under my eyes make them look sunken. The effect I'm going for is something just this side of cadaverous.

> (**ARPEGE** *crosses to* **TRUDY** *and gives her eyes a close inspection. He shakes his head, chews his lips.)*

ARPEGE. Not really seeing it.

> *(Responding to* **TRUDY***'s unhappy reaction.)*

Look, I told you last night that you might want to rethink those two bowls of Rocky Road. Try this: frown.

> (**TRUDY** *obligingly frowns.* **ARPEGE** *shakes his head disapprovingly.)*

> (**TRUDY** *plops down in one of the chairs. She half-groans/half-sighs.)*

TRUDY. I'm *supposed* to be a woman benighted by the shadow of death.

ARPEGE. And yet: are you not still planning to come skipping out here like the "hostess with the mostest"?

TRUDY. I wasn't going to *skip*, Arpege. I was going to *hobble*.

ARPEGE. Maybe you should just keep to your bed.

TRUDY. And let *you* be the one to make the presentation to my Glitter Girls? No, sir. There are far too many working parts to my plan to leave any of this up to you.

    (Beat.)

Anything else?

ARPEGE. *(After a moment's thought.)* After you sit down, don't try to get up without my help, okay? And don't forget to moan and flinch every now and then – you know – on account of all the pain from whatever that disease is you haven't told anybody about yet.

TRUDY. Okay. Is that it?

ARPEGE. *(Shrugging.)* I guess.

TRUDY. *(Getting up.)* Very well then.

    (Looking around.)

Something's missing.

ARPEGE. There's a second tray of canapés. I'll get it.

    *(Something about **ARPEGE**'s nose suddenly captures **TRUDY**'s attention.)*

(Self-conscious.) What?

TRUDY. *(Pointing.)* Darling, you have a very large hardened mucous ball positioned right on the edge of your left –

ARPEGE. *(Translating.)* I have a booger.

    (He gets rid of it.)

It isn't a hard word to say. You might be worth some ungodly fortune, but you and I both know you're still a country girl at heart. Which means you still know words like – oh, if only I could think of one. I know! "*Booger.*"

TRUDY. *(Studying **ARPEGE**'s nose.)* It does now appear to be gone.

ARPEGE. Is this how you treated all the people who worked in your snood factory? Belittling their appearance whenever you got the notion?

TRUDY. No. As a matter of fact, I treated my employees far *worse* than that. Because I expect only the best from the people whom I employ. Unfortunately, they were forever disappointing me. People disappoint me, Arpege, or haven't you noticed? My employees... My family – that is: what little family I have left...

ARPEGE. *(Adding himself to the list.)* ...Your poor maid Arpege. But what about your blessed "Glitter Girls"? Do *they* disappoint you too?

TRUDY. Of course they do.

ARPEGE. And yet you're getting ready to give one of them a ton of money.

TRUDY. Under certain conditions. Run along now. Oh, and bring out the other pitcher of lemonade. Tick-tock, tick-tock!

(**ARPEGE** *starts for the door, stops.*)

ARPEGE. Ma'am?

TRUDY. Yes?

ARPEGE. *(Turning.)* Just what *is* it you're supposed to be dying of? If you're going to tell your guests, don't I have a right to know too?

TRUDY. Well, of course you do. And I wasn't deliberately withholding it from you. It's just that I haven't made up my mind yet. This is no easy task. I require a terminal illness that is very rare and hopefully ungoogleable. I narrowed it down to either "degenerative hypoplasia" or "progressive inversion of the spleen."

ARPEGE. I have no idea what either of those are.

TRUDY. That's because I made them up. I'm hoping that whichever one I pick will sound sufficiently convincing to all my Glitter Girls.

(*Something else about* **ARPEGE**'s *face distracts her.*)

Did you shave this morning?

ARPEGE. By habit I shave only every *other* morning.

TRUDY. I'd rethink that habit.

ARPEGE. *(Sniffing his armpits.)* Do you think I should shower?

TRUDY. When were your last ablutions?

ARPEGE. Sunday.

TRUDY. You're incorrigible. No, no, there isn't time. Go powder yourself and get into your maid's uniform.

ARPEGE. Yes ma'am.

> (*Again,* **ARPEGE** *starts inside. He stops and turns, staring at* **TRUDY**, *apparently wanting to say something to her but not seeming to know how.*)

TRUDY. Is there something you wish to say, Arpege? You have that *look*.

ARPEGE. (*After taking a deep breath to steel himself.*) I don't think what we're doing is right.

TRUDY. Did I ask for your opinion?

ARPEGE. You ask for my opinion twenty times a day, Ms. Tromaine – usually when it comes to things that don't matter a flip. But the important stuff –

TRUDY. Like deciding who I'm going to give my money to?

ARPEGE. I just don't think you're going about this the right way.

TRUDY. Yes, I was starting to get that feeling from you.

ARPEGE. I know it isn't my place to talk you out of this. But I guess I couldn't live with myself if I didn't at least try.

TRUDY. Well, let's consider that you *did* try and you failed.

> (**ARPEGE** *sighs noisily.* **TRUDY** *sits down. She points to the chair directly across from her and indicates that* **ARPEGE** *should do the same.*)

Arpege.

ARPEGE. Yes?

TRUDY. Do you know how much money I made from the sale of my snood factory last month?

ARPEGE. Are you finally going to tell me?

TRUDY. Yes, I'm going to tell you. Fifty – well, closer to fifty-one million dollars.

(**ARPEGE** *whistles.*)

TRUDY. It turns out that I have a real talent for making money. Now, here's the question of the day: do *you* think I should give some of that money to one of my Glitter Girl Sisters of the Gleam and Sparkle?

ARPEGE. Which, hopefully, she'll divide with all the others? Yes, it's a very nice gesture.

(*Beat.*)

Um, are you going to do something nice for your Girl Friday too?

TRUDY. Of course I am! Contingent, of course, on her finally telling me why she had to go undercover.

ARPEGE. I have to tell you that before you leave me any money?

TRUDY. Yes, Arpege. The word of the day is trust. I have put enormous trust in you over the last three years. And you want to know *why*, Arpege? Because you have proven to me your worth and your goodness time and time again. You proved your goodness that day on Highway 27 when you pulled me from my burning Mercedes and dragged me to safety. You risked your own life to save mine, and I remain forever in your debt.

ARPEGE. (*Suddenly abashed.*) Thank you, but it wasn't all me. Part of it was pure adrenaline from those eight cans of Red Bull. But to be honest, I *have* grown a little attached to you.

TRUDY. As I have you.

ARPEGE. But you're having doubts about your Glitter sisters?

TRUDY. Doubts. Yes, that's a good way to put it. Since we all came together sixteen years ago, I've grown fond of them, I'll admit it. And they seem to *adore* me. But is their adoration and devotion – is it genuine, Arpege? Or is it based on the fact that I, say, fly them all to Bermuda once a year for getaway weekends, or get their husbands luxury suites at the Georgia Dome, or pay to send their kids to exclusive boarding schools and prep schools? Do they love me for *me*, Arpege, or are all eight of them –

(*She interrupts herself.*)

Oh, there aren't eight of them anymore, are there? Poor Mary Katherine. Are all *seven* of them just waiting to see how big a chunk of money I might leave them and their families when I kick that ol' bucket? That's what this experiment will prove, in spite of how much you may object to it.

ARPEGE. I promise from now on to keep my objections to myself.

TRUDY. Thank you.

(**ARPEGE** *stands up.*)

ARPEGE. Should we run another check on the listening devices?

TRUDY. I did that already. It was while you were down here straightening the porch. You were humming that Beatles song, weren't you? "Eleanor Rigby."

ARPEGE. Yes, ma'am. And I wasn't humming it very loud, either.

TRUDY. The man at that Atlanta spy store said I was buying the very best bugs on the market. Oh, and I *do not* like that song. It's so bleak.

ARPEGE. I'm trying to put myself in a bleak mood. Isn't this what you want?

TRUDY. Yes, I suppose it is.

ARPEGE. So how much money are you giving to the winner of your game?

TRUDY. I thought sixteen million would be fair. One million for each of the years the Glitter Girls have been glittering. As for the rest of my money, you needn't worry; I plan to be very generous with my maid, chauffeur, cook, and general all-around factotum. In other words, I plan to be very generous with my dear Arpege.

(**ARPEGE** *smiles obscenely.*)

TRUDY. But most will go to the various charities I support. My four ex-husbands can go fly a kite...which they'll have to buy with their own money.

ARPEGE. Not to throw a wrench in your plans, Ms. Tromaine, but is there any chance that you could do for me what you're doing for the winner of your "Glitter Girl Challenge"? Give me my money *before* you check out?

TRUDY. Well, that depends on what kind of naughty business turned you into a fugitive from justice. I certainly don't want to reward criminal behavior.

ARPEGE. Yes, I understand.

TRUDY. Are you ever going to tell me?

ARPEGE. Someday I'll tell you.

TRUDY. But for now we'll just leave things the way they are. Is that what you're saying?

(**ARPEGE** *nods.*)

So you like things right where they are: you and me – our happy little life together?

ARPEGE. It's okay, I guess.

TRUDY. Didn't you once tell me that you've been a woman for so long, it's just a part of who you are now?

ARPEGE. Did I say that? Was I high? Ms. Tromaine, to be honest, I kind of liked being a man. There were certain advantages I really enjoyed.

TRUDY. Well for Heaven's sake, don't tell me those advantages. Considering how hard I had to work as a *woman* to achieve success in the specialized apparel industry, I'd rather not listen to what things were just *handed* to you as part of your male birthright.

ARPEGE. (*Thoroughly chastened.*) Okay. But I was mostly thinking of the convenience of peeing standing up.

(Now **TRUDY** *stands up.*)

TRUDY. I'm glad we had this talk.

ARPEGE. Me too.

TRUDY. *(Looking at her watch.)* Hurry up, now. Go get changed. Check on the bacon puffs. And take the caviar out of the fridge and put it on ice.

ARPEGE. Your guests are having caviar *and* bacon puffs?

TRUDY. Why not? It represents the two epochs of my life. Both the lean years of my hill 'n' holler youth, and the flush years of my late adulthood. Besides, I feel that beluga roe and bacon bits happen to go quite well together.

> (**ARPEGE** *goes inside.* **TRUDY** *finds her tiara and puts it on. She sits down, looking regal and really quite pleased with herself. Lights fade to black.)*

Scene Two

(Twenty-five minutes later.)

(Lights come up on the porch and backyard. **PATTY WESLEY** *and* **CHARLIE SEABURN** *are standing in the herb garden.)*

PATTY. Me too – always the very first. Sometimes I get to parties so early I end up helping the host and hostess put all the food out. Sometimes they send me for ice. But I really can't help myself. My mother says it's because I was born one month premature. There's an irony here, which would be funny if it wasn't so sad.

CHARLIE. You mean the fact that you were born premature and your mother *died* premature?

PATTY. *(Aghast.) No!*

CHARLIE. *(Mortified.)* I can't believe I said that. Sometimes things just fly out of my mouth and I don't know why.

PATTY. Don't worry about it. I remember when we were in high school you hardly let *anything* fly out of your mouth.

CHARLIE. You actually *remember* me from high school?

PATTY. Of course I do. You sat right in front of me in Mr. Higgins' English class and – confession time: sometimes when I'd get bored, I'd study the swirly way the hair grows on the back of your neck.

> *(***CHARLIE*** *slaps his hand over his neck, self-conscious.)*

CHARLIE. Are my swirls, um, *weird*?

PATTY. Not at all. They're *interesting*. They remind me of the swirly sky in that painting, *Starry Night*. Do you know it?

CHARLIE. I'm not sure.

> *(***PATTY*** *pulls out her phone.)*

PATTY. No, what I meant by ironic is that my two brothers were both born *late* and throughout their lives they've always *been* late – I mean for *everything*. Brad was so late for his wedding that Jill – she would have been his first wife – she walked right out on him. He steps inside the church and she's *gone*. I mean *forever*.

CHARLIE. You don't think she was just looking for an excuse not to marry him?

PATTY. Maybe. But he should have called her bluff by showing up on time.

CHARLIE. *(With gentle sarcasm.)* That would have made for a long and happy marriage.

PATTY. *(Showing him the picture she's pulled up on her phone.)* Here it is. Now don't tell me you don't know this painting.

CHARLIE. I *do* know this painting. You should have told me it was by Van Gogh. Van Gogh is my mother's favorite painter. She likes him so much she pronounces his name *Van Gahhck*.

PATTY. I think I knew that about your mother. I know a lot about her, you know. I've been an honorary Glitter Girl since my mom died, and then back in December they officially "legacied" me in. I'm very well-informed about *all* the Glitter Girls.

(With undisguised affection.) It was really sweet of you to come in her place.

CHARLIE. Actually, it was Ms. Tromaine who asked me. She knew that Mama would be in Italy this week. Her Atlanta law firm is opening a branch in Rome.

PATTY. Rome, Italy? Not Rome, Georgia?

CHARLIE. No, I'm pretty sure it's Rome, Italy. Ms. Tromaine said this was going to be an important meeting, so I'm here as Mama's proxy.

(Glancing at the porch.)

Where is everybody?

PATTY. They'll be here. It's still a little early.

(She bends over, rubs her fingers across the needles of a rosemary bush, and sniffs her hand.)

PATTY. I just love this smell. It's so pungent.

> *(She holds her hand out for him to smell, which he does.)*

CHARLIE. *(Nodding.)* So you really liked looking at the back of my neck when we were in high school?

PATTY. *(Teasingly flirty.)* Along with other parts of your anatomy. I have another confession: I love muscular legs on a man. And you always had the nicest legs.

CHARLIE. I guess they *were* kind of sinewy. I ran track.

PATTY. I think I remember that.

> *(Because **CHARLIE** is wearing long pants:)*

And I'll bet you *still* have beautiful, sinewy legs. I hope I'm not making you blush.

CHARLIE. I don't blush. Thank you for the compliment. I think you have nice boobs.

PATTY. *(Caught off-guard.)* Did you just say what I think you just said?

CHARLIE. *(Mortified again.)* Oh man. I can't believe I –

PATTY. You don't have a filter, do you? Some men don't.

CHARLIE. Oh God. Oh God.

PATTY. *(Disarmingly.)* I'll take it as the compliment you intended.

CHARLIE. Thank you. Let's change the subject. Better yet – I think I just heard a car door slam. Maybe we should go back to the porch.

> *(**CHARLIE** and **PATTY** cross to the porch and climb the stairs. **PATTY** goes to her bag, takes out her tiara, and puts it on.)*

That looks nice.

PATTY. It's my "legacy" tiara. It belonged to my mother. Where's *your* mother's?

CHARLIE. In my backpack. But I have no plans to wear my mother's tiara, no matter how funny she thought it might be.

PATTY. That's a shame. It would have been fun to see what you'd look like as a Glitter Girl.

CHARLIE. Sorry to disappoint you, but that ain't happening.

> *(**VALERIE FAIRHOPE** and **FLOSSIE PRICE** are led out onto the porch by **ARPEGE**, who is now wearing an over-the-top French maid's outfit. Both **VALERIE** and **FLOSSIE** wear their tiaras.)*

FLOSSIE. Hey, Patty-cake!

PATTY. Hi, Flossie.

> *(**FLOSSIE** gives **PATTY** a big hug.)*

VALERIE. *(To **PATTY**, indicating **CHARLIE**.)* Nobody said we could bring dates.

PATTY. Are you getting senile, Valerie? This is Barbara's son: Charlie.

VALERIE. *(Squinting at **CHARLIE**.)* Not Charlie *Seaburn*!

> *(She takes out her glasses, gives **CHARLIE** a look, then puts them away. Note: this will be a habit of **VALERIE**'s which the actor playing her should feel free to have fun with throughout the play. Think: Marilyn Monroe in* How to Marry a Millionaire.*)*

Of course I know Charlie.

*(To **CHARLIE**.)* Although I might have recognized you sooner if you'd been wearing your track shorts. Where's your mom?

CHARLIE. She's in Rome, Ms. Fairhope.

FLOSSIE. Is that Rome, Georgia – or the other one where spaghetti comes from?

CHARLIE. Rome, Italy, Ms. Price.

VALERIE. Your mom's gotten to be the real globe-trotter, hasn't she?

CHARLIE. Her firm is going international. They're exploring the possibility of a big merger, but I'm not supposed to talk about it.

VALERIE. Then why are you talking about it?

PATTY. *(Having fun.)* Charlie has no filter. He opens his mouth and things just pop out.

FLOSSIE. Are you gonna be a lawyer like your ma?

CHARLIE. That's the plan.

FLOSSIE. Well that ain't gonna be too good don'tcha think – standin' in front of a jury and things just poppin' out?

CHARLIE. *(Good-naturedly.)* No, I suppose that could be a problem. Which is why I don't plan on being a litigator.

VALERIE. *(Looking him up and down.)* I'm not happy being the one to break it to you, Charlie-o, but this meeting is supposed to be just for us Glitter Girls. At least that's what I was told. I thought we were only making one exception and that was for Mary Katherine's husband Dowd. I think it's because poor M.K. is still warm in the ground, and Trudy wanted to be nice.

FLOSSIE. *(Chiding.)* That was just plumb rude, Val!

VALERIE. How would *you* have said it, Flossie? Do you mountain people have some better way to speak of the recently dead?

FLOSSIE. Well, we don't *disrespect* 'em.

PATTY. *(Lightheartedly.)* That's okay, Flossie. Valerie disrespects everyone.

(To **VALERIE**.*)* It just so happens, Val, that Charlie is *supposed* to be here.

FLOSSIE. *(To* **VALERIE**.*)* In other words, sugar-cake: why don't mind your own cotton-pickin' business?

(Turning to **ARPEGE**.*)* Arpege, are we gonna get to see Trudy down here on the porch, or will we be takin' turns visiting her up in her sick room?

ARPEGE. She'd *prefer* to come down. I mean, if she's feeling up to it.

(We hear the sound of a doorbell from offstage.)

More Glitter Girls. Excuse me.

(He exits into the house.)

PATTY. *(To* **FLOSSIE.***)* Is Trudy pretty bad off?

FLOSSIE. *(Nodding.)* The last time I talked to her she said she'd gotten some discouragin' news from her doctor.

VALERIE. How discouraging?

FLOSSIE. Whatever it is she's got, I think it's gettin' worse.

VALERIE. What do you mean: *whatever it is she's got*? Didn't she tell you what's wrong with her?

FLOSSIE. Everybody knows Trudy's a private person. She don't go tellin' people things lessin' she's got a good reason.

VALERIE. But reading between the lines, do you think it's *terminal*?

FLOSSIE. I'm guessin' if it's gotten worse, then there's that possibility, y'all.

PATTY. I'll bet that's why she summoned us all here. She wants to give everybody the bad news at the same time.

FLOSSIE. I just don't understand it. Trudy was the picture of health when we all got together around the holidays.

VALERIE. Sometimes these things can sneak up on you. Back when I was a dancer –

FLOSSIE. Now don't you go tellin' us one of your gross stripper stories, Valerie.

VALERIE. *(Ignoring this.)* One of the dancers, see – she found out she had worms.

FLOSSIE. Oh sweet Jesus, Valerie, you hush up!

VALERIE. And it wasn't the kind of worms you can get rid of very easily.

FLOSSIE. Could you please shut your dad-burned pie hole, Valerie?

*(***MAYVONNE RAUSCH** *steps out onto the porch.)*

MAYVONNE. Why does Valerie have to shut her pie hole?

PATTY. Hi, Mayvonne. You don't want to know.

MAYVONNE. *(Just noticing* **CHARLIE.***)* Why, look what the cat dragged in! I spy with my little eye: little Charlie Seaburn, looking healthy and spry!

CHARLIE. Afternoon, Ms. Rausch.

MAYVONNE. Oh please call me Mayvonne. I'm not your seventh grade teacher anymore. And just look at *you*! Barbara Seaburn's little boy all grown up.

VALERIE. *(Mock-confidential to* **MAYVONNE**.*)* He looks even better in shorts and a muscle-tee.

MAYVONNE. Would you listen to yourself, Valerie? You're old enough to be the boy's mother.

FLOSSIE. *(Confidentially to* **PATTY**.*)* There's a story that's been goin' around for years that Valerie *is* Charlie's mother. That she had him out of wedlock and Barbara asked if she could adopt him because she wanted a baby, but unfortunately her womb wouldn't fix.

CHARLIE. Ms. Price, I actually heard every word of that. And there's no truth to that story at all.

MAYVONNE. I don't know how rumors like that get started.

FLOSSIE. *I* do. Valerie makes it purdy easy. She's a big ol' skank.

VALERIE. Flossie Price, if you don't watch your mouth I could start a rumor right now – all about your dentist husband and that chesty new hygienist of his.

FLOSSIE. I'm sorry, Val. I didn't mean to call you a big ol' skank. You did, after all, lose some of that pig fat of yours with all that Zumba-ing you've been doin'. Now you're more like a *Size Six* skank.

MAYVONNE. Ladies, please! Show some decorum. We have gathered at the home of a woman who probably isn't long for this earth. Please try to be respectful.

PATTY. *(To* **MAYVONNE**.*)* So, do *you* think that's why she called this meeting?

(**MAYVONNE** *nods sadly.*)

CHARLIE. Mama wonders if all this might have something to do with the will Ms. Tromaine's drawing up.

MAYVONNE. Your mother isn't handling Trudy's will?

CHARLIE. *(Shaking his head.)* She's using Mama's law firm, but there's actually a different partner taking care of the will.

VALERIE. I'd take that as a good sign.

MAYVONNE. What do you mean?

VALERIE. That Trudy might be planning on leaving something to Charlie's mother. I'll bet she's trying to avoid a conflict of interest. And if something's coming to Barbara, then more than likely, something's coming to all the rest of us too.

FLOSSIE. With all that circlin' and circlin', Valerie, don't your vulture wings ever get tired?

VALERIE. *(Defensive.)* I am only making a logical observation. Do you want me to just sit here and not make a peep?

FLOSSIE. You mean I don't have to pray on that anymore?

> *(**MAMIE EWING** now appears at the door, unaccompanied and unnoticed by those on the porch. She stands on the threshold, listening. **MAMIE** wears her tiara.)*

VALERIE. *(Dropping her voice and speaking "entre nous.")* Do *you* think I'm being – what's the word, Mayvonne?

MAYVONNE. Ghoulish?

VALERIE. That's right. Do *you* think it's ghoulish just to get some kind of idea as to what Trudy's plans might be?

MAMIE. *(Overhearing the question and jumping in.)* Well, *I* don't think you're being ghoulish at all. I've been wondering the very same thing.

> *(Everyone turns to **MAMIE**, who greets her fellow Glitter Girls with a big smile.)*

FLOSSIE. Hello, Mamie. It's right nice to see you.

MAMIE. But you just saw me at my dress shop on Friday.

FLOSSIE. That don't count. You were tied up with a customer. I had to be waited on by that flibbertigibbet girl with the crossed eyes.

VALERIE. I have a problem with that girl myself. I'm always thinking: is she looking at *me* or is she checking the weather out the window?

MAMIE. It so happens that Carolee is my best sales clerk. She can't help the fact that her eyes go off in two different directions.

VALERIE. *(To* **MAMIE.***)* You know something else I have a problem with when it comes to that store of yours?

MAMIE. Oh please, Valerie, must we? Whatever it is, I'm sure you've mentioned it before.

VALERIE. Maybe Charlie doesn't know.

CHARLIE. That's okay. I don't have to know.

VALERIE. *(Undaunted.)* It's the name you gave that damned place. Whoever heard of a dress shop called "No Wire Hangers"?

MAMIE. *I* didn't name it that! It was what the store was called when I bought it from Lance Lassiter. I just thought it would be best to keep the name for the sake of customer continuity.

MAYVONNE. In Mamie's defense, she did take down all those angry Joan Crawford posters. To be honest, it was always very hard trying on foundation garments with Joan Crawford looking like she wanted a piece of me.

MAMIE. *(Looking about.)* Who isn't here? Where's Mary Katherine?

FLOSSIE. With Jesus, would be my guess.

MAMIE. *(Mortified.)* Oh, I can't believe I –

VALERIE. It might have helped you to remember that M.K. died last month if you'd bothered to come to her funeral.

MAMIE. I'm sorry I missed Mary Katherine's funeral but it couldn't be helped. That was the day of the big Republican Party picnic and you know how Dean likes me to be with him when he has to press the flesh.

MAYVONNE. So it's official: your husband is running for mayor.

MAMIE. He won't be making his formal announcement until next week, but...*yes.*

> *(Looking around.)*

Where's Corinne? In the bathroom?

PATTY. She called me and said she was running late.

> (**FLOSSIE** *starts to cry. She whips out a handkerchief.*)

(Misinterpreting the tears.) I'm sure she'll get here eventually, Flossie.

FLOSSIE. Land sakes! I'm not cryin' about Corinne. I'm cryin' for Trudy. This just might be the last time we'll all be together. Maybe she called us all here to tell us goodbye. Do you know how many years we've been together?

MAMIE. Fifteen?

FLOSSIE. *Sixteen.*

> *(Indicating* **PATTY** *and* **CHARLIE.**)

These two over here were just startin' first grade.

> *(She blows her nose. It's a real honker.)*

And me and Trudy go back even farther than that. We both came from the hills. My holler was just three hollers over from her holler. We was both so poor, I don't think neither of us put on our first pair of shoes until we was old enough to sprout the nipple buds.

MAYVONNE. *(Chastising, regarding* **CHARLIE.**) Flossie! There is a man present.

CHARLIE. *(Shrugging.)* It's okay. I have no idea what nipple buds are.

FLOSSIE. All's I'm sayin' is that I think of Trudy as my very own sister. Don't matter that she's gotten all high falutin' over the years, and as mean as a mongrel she-bitch. I happen to know that deep down inside her there's still that sweet barefoot country girl I used to know.

VALERIE. Well, I just hope that when it comes to giving away all that money, it'll be the sweet country girl doing it, and not the mongrel she-bitch.

> *(There is no time for anyone to respond. A rustle at the door turns everyone's heads to* **ARPEGE** *and* **CORINNE CULVERT.** **CORINNE**'s *face and clothes are blotched and glopped with what looks like white goop.* **ARPEGE** *carries a bath towel over his arm like a maître d' at a fancy restaurant.)*

CORINNE. Hi, everybody. I rear-ended a cement mixer.

ARPEGE. I'm going to take Corinne out to the side yard and hose her down.

> *(We hear a doorbell ring from inside the house.)*

(Shouting through the door.) Come on in! Front door's unlocked!

(To the others.) That's probably Mr. Foster.

> **(ARPEGE** *leads* **CORINNE** *down the stairs into the backyard. Once in the yard,* **ARPEGE** *takes* **CORINNE** *offstage.* **DOWD FOSTER** *comes out onto the porch from inside the house.)*

DOWD. Hello, everyone.

> *(Ad-libbed greetings for* **DOWD,** *after which:)*

MAYVONNE. It's so nice to see you here, Dowd. I know you haven't been getting around much since the funeral.

DOWD. I just haven't felt much like going out.

FLOSSIE. You haven't gotten back to work yet, honey?

DOWD. *(Shaking his head.)* I've got a really good crew working for me at the tire store. They're doing just fine without me.

MAMIE. How's Darlene getting along?

DOWD. She misses her mother something awful. She isn't crying so much anymore, though. Or maybe she's just trying really hard *not* to cry when she brings David and Jessie over to see their grandpa.

MAMIE. *(To* **DOWD.***)* You tell Darlene to come down to the dress shop and pick herself out something really nice.

DOWD. I will. Thank you, Mamie.

MAYVONNE. *(To* **DOWD.***)* We're all so happy you're here.

DOWD. It's good to see all of you. I needed to get out, I know it. I've been spending too much time watching TV, Darlene says. Of course, it's mostly shows that remind me of Mary Katherine. She liked this one show where it's about people looking at beach houses they might like to buy. Mary Katherine loved the ocean. But when things got really bad – right there near the end, she stopped watching pretty much everything. Well, *almost* everything. The only thing she wanted to look at in the hospice was the *Puppy Bowl*. See, every year for quite a few years I'd tape those *Puppy Bowl* broadcasts that came on during the Super Bowl. Well, I'd put in one of those *Puppy Bowl* videotapes and we'd watch those little furballs, nipping and yipping and tumbling all around, and we'd be laughing and crying at the same time, like a couple of crazy people.

> *(***DOWD*** addresses the wet corners of his eyes with a forefinger.* ***MAYVONNE*** *comforts him in silence by placing a gentle hand on his shoulder.)*

FLOSSIE. *(Privately to* **VALERIE.***)* What's the *Puppy Bowl*?

VALERIE. It's puppies rolling all around on something that looks like a miniature football field.

FLOSSIE. Well, I'll be! I didn't even know we had this option.

MAYVONNE. *(To* **DOWD.***)* Anyway, I think it's a good thing you're out and about. Do you like bacon puffs? There's a tray of them over there.

> *(***DOWD*** nods.)*

PATTY. *(To* **DOWD.***)* You know, if Darlene was interested, she could become a legacy Glitter Girl like me. Isn't that right, Mamie?

MAMIE. *(Put on the spot, she responds graciously.)* Well, I don't see why not.

VALERIE. *(To* **FLOSSIE.***)* You think the Glitter Girls will stay together after Trudy goes?

FLOSSIE. I don't want to think about losing Trudy.

MAMIE. I vote that no matter what happens, we keep the gang together.

MAYVONNE. That *would* be nice. Not that we don't have our differences from time to time, but I still think we get along pretty well, all things considered.

MAMIE. Where's your tiara, Mayvonne? You're the only Glitter Girl out here who's not glittering.

MAYVONNE. I'm sorry. I just forgot.

> *(She finds her tiara and puts it on.)*

FLOSSIE. *(To* **MAYVONNE.***)* Wearin' the diadem oughta be a matter of pride.

MAYVONNE. I said I just forgot, Flossie.

FLOSSIE. *(Educating* **CHARLIE.***)* This here tiara binds us all like glue, you see.

> *(To* **MAYVONNE,** *regarding her tiara.)* You got it on a little crooked there, honey.

> *(She fixes* **MAYVONNE***'s tiara and takes a step back.)*

Now don't you look a picture?

> *(***MAYVONNE** *grins self-consciously from the compliment.)*

MAMIE. *(Pointing to* **FLOSSIE** *and* **VALERIE,** *who stand together.)* Now here's your *picture*, ladies. I present to you: Flossie and Floozie.

> *(Everyone reacts with mirth except for* **VALERIE.***)*

VALERIE. You're one to talk, Mamie. How many husbands did you run through before you settled on Dean?

MAMIE. Three. But in my own defense: the first one died. The second one cheated. And the third one snored like a cement mixer.

MAYVONNE. Speaking of cement mixer, I hope that Arpege can get Corinne hosed down before all that concrete sets. I have never in my life known a woman as unlucky as poor Corinne.

PATTY. But at least so far as her marriage goes, she and Dabney seem to be working things out. Corinne told me that he hasn't had a drop to drink in three weeks. I think he's even started to go to AA.

VALERIE. Now, if he can only get a job.

> (**CORINNE** *and* **ARPEGE** *return to the backyard from the side yard.* **CORINNE** *is wet. She is wrapped in the bath towel. She shivers. They mount the stairs to the porch, everyone stepping back to let them pass.*)

ARPEGE. *(Formally.)* We're going to get Corinne into some warm clothes and once that's done I'll check in with Trudy and see if she'll come down and visit with everybody for a few minutes.

MAMIE. If that's an inconvenience, we'll be happy to come upstairs and gather around her deathbed.

MAYVONNE. *(Appalled.)* Mamie Ewing, did you actually just say "deathbed"?

MAMIE. *(Appalled at herself.)* That didn't come out at *all* the way I meant it.

> (**ARPEGE**, *privately amused, shakes his head. He and* **CORINNE** *go inside.*)

CHARLIE. I have that problem too: saying things aloud that I ought to just be thinking.

PATTY. *(Explaining.)* Charlie doesn't have a filter.
(To **CHARLIE**, *charitably.)* Of course, there are far worse faults a person could have.

VALERIE. *(Looking right at* **MAMIE**.*)* You *could* be a serial divorcée.

MAMIE. *(Glaring right back at* **VALERIE**.*)* Or a serial *slut.*

*(On **VALERIE**'s offended reaction, snidely:)*

MAMIE. Did I actually say that out loud? Looks like Charlie and me really *are* two peas in a pod.

MAYVONNE. When you get to be *my* age saying improper things from time to time just goes with the territory. There are a few women I visit at the assisted living center in my neighborhood, and, why, they're just as sweet as can be, but sometimes right out of the blue they'll say things that will make your hair stand on end.

MAMIE. Mayvonne, please tell us you're not going to offer examples.

MAYVONNE. Oh my good Lord! I couldn't repeat some of those things if you paid me!

VALERIE. Mayvonne Rausch, you aren't going to sit *[Or stand; whatever applies.]* there and tell me that you have never in your life had a need to use profanity.

MAYVONNE. *(Thinking back.)* Well, there was that *one* time. But I had a very good excuse. Linda was presenting breech and my hippie-dippy sister – she was calling herself "Clover" at the time. "Clover" decided that being a doula, she knew everything in the world there was to know about childbirth.

CHARLIE. What's a doula?

PATTY. It's a woman who assists a midwife.

*(**CHARLIE** nods.)*

MAYVONNE. Anyway, she'd read, I guess, in the *Dr. Spock Special Edition for Hippie Mothers* that a baby can turn itself around all by itself if you play music to it, and so this is what "Clover" – she was actually born Jeannine – Jeannine forces me to do: sit there and let her play records right between my legs. "Lollypop." "Ragdoll." "My Guy." And my fetal daughter doesn't seem to be moving even an inch, and pretty soon I'd simply had enough of this nonsense. I think the final straw was when Jeannine put on that record of the Animals singing, "I'm Crying." "I'm crying. Hear me crying, baby!" Well, I just let fly the kinds of words that would straighten a sailor's curlies. I made her drive me right then and there to the obstetrician and, thank Jesus, everything worked out. As it turned out, I didn't even need a Caesarian.

(*A short, awkward silence ensues.*)

Was that "TMI"?

FLOSSIE. That was an awful lot of "I," darlin'.

MAMIE. In any event, I really do apologize for saying that Trudy is on her deathbed, though you all know you were thinking the same thing: that our friend Trudy probably *is* getting herself ready for last rites.

FLOSSIE. (*Privately to* **VALERIE.**) What's "last rites"?

VALERIE. It's a Catholic thing. I think the priest shakes something over your head and talks in Latin and then you die.

MAYVONNE. I think it might be a good idea if we stop imagining what might be going on here and just take our seats and wait for Trudy to come down and explain. I'm sure that once she makes her appearance, she'll probably prefer we didn't look like we're all about to head off to her funeral.

(*Everyone chooses a chair,* **PATTY** *and* **CHARLIE**'s *right next to each other.*)

PATTY. (*Teasingly, to* **CHARLIE.**) You sure you don't want to put on that tiara? It'll be fun.

CHARLIE. Not for the person wearing it.

DOWD. (*Seriously.*) Is that what we're supposed to do? Wear the tiaras? I brought Mary Katherine's.

(*He pulls it out. He puts it on his head. He doesn't smile. He just stares ahead, wearing the tiara, obviously deep in thought about his late wife. Everyone sits in silence, respectful of Dowd's decision to be still and quiet. The silence is broken by* **CORINNE** *coming out of the house. She is now dry and wearing different clothes – very nice clothes, no doubt* *belonging to Trudy. She goes to an empty chair next to **VALERIE** and sits down. After a silence:)*

VALERIE. *(To **CORINNE**.)* I saw you at the Publix the other day. You were standing at the hot food bar.

CORINNE. It was Campbell's birthday. She likes Chinese food, so I was getting her some Kung Pao chicken.

VALERIE. I would have said hello, but I was stuck in the checkout line, and after I finished checking out, you'd moved on to some other part of the store.

(An empty silence passes.)

Was it good? The Kung Pao chicken?

CORINNE. It was okay. Campbell liked it.

VALERIE. That's good.

*(Another silence, which **FLOSSIE** purposefully breaks:)*

FLOSSIE. There was this one time I was standin' in line at the Publix, and the woman in front of me had just been to the hot food bar, and she took this plastic container out of her basket and you wouldn't believe what was in it.

VALERIE. We give up.

FLOSSIE. All's that was inside was one single, solitary green bean. I looked right at that green bean and I said, "Excuse me, ma'am, but it do appear that you're only buying one green bean and inquirin' minds would want to know why." And she goes, "My daughter hates green beans but I know they're good for her, so we've decided to approach this problem *incrementally.*"

VALERIE. She actually used the word "incrementally"?

FLOSSIE. *(Nodding.)* I couldn't believe it. She was wearing a "Hello, Kitty" t-shirt.

*(**ARPEGE** and **TRUDY**, who wears a satiny quilted bed robe as well as her tiara, come out onto the porch. **TRUDY** looks wan and tired, but nowhere near "cadaverous.")*

TRUDY. Hello, everyone.

> *(Regarding all the tiaras.)*

Well, look at all that "gleam and sparkle"!

> *(Ad-libbed greetings for* **TRUDY**. **ARPEGE** *leads* **TRUDY** *to the remaining empty chair on the porch. He helps her ease herself down into it.)*

Thank you, Arpege.

(Mock-confidential to the others.) My maid has big strong arms.

> *(Polite nods all around.)*

(Getting down to business.) It's so nice you all could make it.

VALERIE. Barbara didn't come. She's in Rome.

TRUDY. Yes, I know. Hello, Charlie. I think the last time I saw you was when I flew everybody up to New York to see *Hamilton*. Oh, how I loved all of our big Glitter Girl family excursions.

> *(Nods of agreement all around.)*

Of course, I'm sure you all have much better things to do this Wednesday afternoon than come visit your poor, sick friend Trudy. And on such short notice.

> *(Obligatory ad-libbed protests.)*

(To **ARPEGE**.*)* I think I'll have one of those crackers.

> *(**ARPEGE** follows her pointed finger to the tray with the hors d'oeuvres.)*

No, not that one. One of the ones with the cream cheese and capers. Yes, right there!

(As **ARPEGE** *takes her the cracker.)* And some of that lemonade. Thank you.

(As she begins to nibble.) As you all have, no doubt, guessed, I'm not doing very well. The doctors aren't very encouraging.

FLOSSIE. *(Devastated.)* Oh sweet Lord, it's exactly what we thought!

TRUDY. Now don't you start crying, Flossie, because all the Kleenex boxes are upstairs.

> (**ARPEGE** *gives* **TRUDY** *her glass of lemonade.*)

(To **ARPEGE***.)* Thank you.

(Back to **FLOSSIE***.)* You have to be brave. Just like that time when we were girls and everyone laughed at you at the barn dance because you danced like a marionette.

FLOSSIE. *(Nodding.)* It was so hurtful. But I didn't cry, no ma'am.

> (**TRUDY** *smiles affectionately. She reaches out to take* **FLOSSIE***'s hand, but because* **FLOSSIE** *isn't sitting right next to her* **FLOSSIE** *has to get partially out of her chair and stretch toward* **TRUDY***, like she's playing Twister, to make the connection.*)

TRUDY. *(Shrugging.)* One month. Two months. Or for all anyone knows, I could drop dead this weekend. No one can ever be sure when it comes to a rare disease that hasn't been very well studied.

MAYVONNE. So that's what you have? A rare disease?

> (**TRUDY** *nods.*)

MAMIE. Is there a name for it?

> (**ARPEGE** *narrows his eyes on* **TRUDY***, obviously curious to know which of the two possibilities she has decided to go with.*)

TRUDY. It's called "progressive inversion of the spleen." Don't bother to look it up. It's so rare there's hardly any literature about it.

MAYVONNE. Dear, what does that mean: "progressive inversion of the spleen"?

VALERIE. *(Volunteering an answer on* **TRUDY***'s behalf.)* Well, Mayvonne, it obviously means that her spleen has been, you know, *inverted.*

FLOSSIE. *(Helpfully.)* And that it probably gets more and more inverted each day. Am I right, Trudy?

(**TRUDY** *nods.*)

CHARLIE. *(Sitting forward; this apparently interests him.)* That sounds more like a condition than a disease.

TRUDY. *(Quickly.)* It's both a condition *and* a disease.

MAMIE. And it can kill a person?

TRUDY. That's the official prognosis.

CHARLIE. What does the spleen *do*, anyway?

DOWD. It's works with the human immune system. It removes old blood cells and recycles iron.

VALERIE. How is it you know so much about the spleen?

DOWD. When I was in high school, one of my buddies on the football team ended up at the bottom of one of those "pile-on" tackles and his spleen ruptured. The doctors had to remove it.

FLOSSIE. You can take out a spleen?

DOWD. Yes, you can.

(*To* **TRUDY**.) Why aren't the doctors recommending that *your* spleen be removed?

TRUDY. *(Fumbling a little.)* Well, normally that wouldn't be a problem. But there are dangerous complications when a spleen is – you know – *inverted.*

FLOSSIE. And getting more inverted every day.

MAYVONNE. Good mercy! And there's nothing else that can be done?

TRUDY. Nothing that they've been able to come up with.

FLOSSIE. It's a death sentence! It's an absolute death sentence!

(**FLOSSIE** *is starting to get weepy again.*)

MAYVONNE. Oh Trudy, sweetie, our hearts go out to you.

VALERIE. *All* of our hearts. The hearts of everyone on this porch, all of whom love you...*equally.*

(*There are a few suspicious looks thrown* **VALERIE**'s *way. Is this about Trudy's money?*)

TRUDY. Thank you. Your friendship means so much to me. That's why...

(Steadying herself for what is to come.)

TRUDY. ...That's why it pains me to put you through all this.

MAYVONNE. Don't you worry about us.

TRUDY. No, what I mean is: it pains me to put you through what I'm *getting ready* to put you all through. Today. This afternoon.

MAMIE. Trudy, dear, what are you talking about?

TRUDY. I have decided, Mamie, that rather than bless all of my Glitter Girl sisters with the fruits – well, *some* of the fruits – of my many years of hard labor, I'd rather leave that part of my fortune – sixteen million dollars to be exact – to just *one* of you. One of the eight of you who just happen to be sitting on this porch.

VALERIE. Now, wait a minute –

FLOSSIE. Let her finish, Valerie.

VALERIE. No, no, no, no. Just a minute.

FLOSSIE. You hush up, Val, and let Trudy say what she came down here to say. We're all listenin', Trudy. Go on with your speech.

TRUDY. Thank you, Flossie. I have chosen, in spite of how much I love all of you – a love that I've demonstrated to you on countless occasions these last sixteen years – I've chosen to now be somewhat *less* generous as I make that final, permanent transition. I plan, ladies...
(In deference to **CHARLIE** *and* **DOWD**.*)* and *gentlemen*, to bestow the big prize singularly – not –

(Turning to **MAYVONNE**.*)*

What?

MAYVONNE. Severally.

TRUDY. Yes. Severally. Not that this lucky person may not feel it in her – or *his* heart – to share their good fortune with the rest of you, but that's entirely up to her...or him.

(She takes a breath, then another.)

ARPEGE. *(The nurse.)* Do you need your pills?

TRUDY. No, I'll be all right. I just need a moment.

(She holds out her hand. **ARPEGE** *rushes over to take it.)*

ARPEGE. *(To the others.)* She's so brave. She's the bravest woman I ever met.

TRUDY. *(Letting go of* **ARPEGE***'s hand.)* Thank you, Arpege. You give me strength.

*(***ARPEGE** *nods nobly.)*

MAMIE. So are you going to tell us who this one lucky person is, or do we have to wait for the reading of the will?

PATTY. *(Sarcastic.)* Could you try that again, Mamie? But make it a little snottier next time.

MAMIE. I was *not* being – Now just who are *you* to be talking to me like this? You're a *legacy* G.G.!

VALERIE. *(To* **PATTY.***)* Mamie voted against the idea of having legacy Glitter Girls. She was actually the only one of us who did.

FLOSSIE. Are y'all finished? Trudy looks like she has somethin' else she wants to say. You go right ahead, Trudy. We're listenin'.

TRUDY. I was going to say – and this is the most important part – that *I* won't be the one to pick. Instead, you'll be making this decision yourselves.

MAYVONNE. I don't understand.

VALERIE. We don't understand.

TRUDY. I mean that you – all of you – will be choosing the one among you most deserving of sixteen million of my snood dollars. That person will be free to share that money with the rest of you, or to keep it all to herself, if this be the lucky recipient's choice.

(She takes a deep breath.)

There. Now, I have to go upstairs and take my meds and get some rest. I feel like I've just been run over by a bus. Arpege will be standing by if anyone needs anything. I'll come back down when she reports to me that you've made your decision.

MAMIE. *Really*, Trudy? Something as important as what's going to happen to a big part of your fortune and we must turn this into some kind of back-porch reality show?

TRUDY. *(After a dramatic beat.)* Yes.

>   *(She signals for* ARPEGE *to help her up from the big chair, which he does.)*

I really think this is the best way. I happen to know that some of you clearly don't deserve this money. You see: I've found out things about you – some of you – well, sadly: *most* of you – things that disappoint and depress me. It's very hard for me to put it all on a scale. I choose to let *you* do that. All I ask is that when you're done, you present me with the name of one person, so that when I meet with my lawyer tomorrow, *that* will be the name that will go into my will.

MAYVONNE. *(Sadly.)* Do we really disappoint you that much, Trudy?

TRUDY. Of course you do, Mayvonne. But that doesn't mean I don't forgive even the worst of you. You're all human. And humans have faults. I probably have worse faults than all of you. But fate has left me – as flawed as *I* am – in possession of all this money, and so this is the only course I've come up with for how to dispose of it fairly – as far-fetched as all of this may sound. Arpege, give them the bell.

>   (ARPEGE *pulls out a hotel bell – the kind that "tings" when you tap the knob at the top with your palm. He places it on the table.)*

Anything you need, just tap this bell and Arpege will come and see to it.

>   (ARPEGE *takes* TRUDY *into the house. Their exit from the porch is followed by stunned silence.)*

MAMIE. I could not have predicted something like this in a million years.

CORINNE. Do you think it's some kind of a practical joke?

VALERIE. Why would a woman who's *that* sick want to play a joke like that?

PATTY. Trudy always *has* had a very strange sense of humor.

MAYVONNE. I think the only thing we can do is assume that this *isn't* a joke and do what she asks. Of course, the big question is: how do we even begin to do what she wants?

DOWD. I suppose we can always just put it to a vote.

VALERIE. Excuse me, but I vote that we *don't* put it to a vote. At least not right away. Trudy said that she found out things about us. Maybe these are things we ought to know about each other – things that just might influence our decision.

MAMIE. Valerie's probably right.

PATTY. Maybe what we ought to do is: instead of taking one big vote, we take a series of little votes – narrowing our choices down. Like they do on those – well, those reality TV shows.

MAYVONNE. I'm not comfortable with this.

VALERIE. If that's the case, Mayvonne, then maybe you might want to think about leaving the island.

PATTY. This isn't an island, Val. It's a porch.

MAYVONNE. Well, I don't plan to sit here and listen to y'all saying nasty things about each other. And I can *certainly* do without a bunch of blackball votes like we're some coven of Middle School Mean Girls. I'd much rather just go home.

PATTY. Please don't go home, Mayvonne. We'll get this worked out.

CHARLIE. Mayvonne, I really have to agree with Patty.

> (**CHARLIE** *and* **PATTY** *exchange mutually supportive smiles.*)

Doing this using some kind of elimination process probably is the best way. And it won't be as bad as you think. Look, we all can agree that the right thing to do is for the person we pick to share that money with the rest of us. So this really isn't even about picking the most deserving person, moneywise. It's about choosing the person we most trust to serve *everybody's* best interests.

PATTY. *(With an admiring smile.)* I think you're going to make an excellent lawyer.

CHARLIE. Thanks.

CORINNE. I happen to think we're *all* honest and trustworthy. If our biggest problem is how to whittle ourselves down – well, I don't think that's such a terrible problem to have.

VALERIE. Corinne, sweetie, you need to pull your head out of the cement mixer. Trudy was right. There are things that each of us has done that we're not proud of – things that might come out – that maybe *need* to come out – if we're going to do our jobs right.

MAYVONNE. Then you're making my point. Excuse me. I'd like to go home now.

FLOSSIE. Mayvonne, honey, instead of going home, why don't you just take yourself off the porch and go sit somewhere in the backyard – someplace nice and shady and good-smelling and we'll come get you once we've made our decision? What do you think about that?

MAYVONNE. I suppose I could sit in the herb garden. It's so fragrant and the smells are so exotic.

VALERIE. You do that, Mayvonne. Somebody get Mayvonne's chair and park her in the herb garden where she doesn't have to be a party to any of this.

> *(**CHARLIE** and **DOWD** both go for **MAYVONNE**'s chair at the same time. After a brief tussle, **DOWD** gives it up to **CHARLIE**.)*

MAYVONNE. But don't y'all be talking too loud, because I don't care to know any of your dark secrets.

MAMIE. *(Wryly.)* If there's some secret that has to be revealed, we'll make sure to keep our voices to an appalled whisper.

MAYVONNE. Are you making fun of me, Mamie?

MAMIE. Of course I am, dear. Because you're being awfully silly about this. Charlie, put that chair down.

(**CHARLIE** *doesn't put the chair down.*)

Now Mayvonne, you know how fond we all are of each other and how long we've known each other, and I do not believe that we can't just talk this out in a way that doesn't have to get anyone needlessly upset.

VALERIE. *(With a skeptical sneer.)* Uh-huh.

FLOSSIE. Can we put a muzzle on Valerie? That might help too.

VALERIE. *(Relenting.)* I promise to behave.

MAMIE. Good. Charlie, put Mayvonne's chair down.

CHARLIE. Mayvonne, do you want me to take your chair to the herb garden or leave it here?

MAYVONNE. I'll stay put for now.

(Suddenly stern.) But everybody better mind their p's and q's, I'm not kidding.

CHARLIE. *(Setting the chair down.)* Now *that* takes me back.

MAYVONNE. Takes you back to what?

CHARLIE. To those times in seventh grade when you had to leave the room and you'd read us all the riot act. I swear, Mayvonne, you had a real knack for putting the fear of God into a whole room full of thirteen-year-olds.

MAYVONNE. *(Wistful.)* The fire, alas, has burned itself out. I am just a shell of the dragon lady I once was.

PATTY. Well, we love you just the same.

(**PATTY** *hugs* **MAYVONNE**.)

VALERIE. Does anyone want to say anything before we take our first elimination vote?

CORINNE. Oh. We're already starting? Can I pee first?

FLOSSIE. *(Raising her hand.)* Me too.

MAMIE. Do the two of you think this is going to be a long process?

CORINNE. *(Matter-of-factly.)* We *do*, Mamie. We think this could be a *very* long process. I should probably call home and tell Dabney to make some SpaghettiOs for him and the girls. That's the only meal he knows how to make.

> *(**CORINNE** exits into the house.)*

CHARLIE. I probably should call my mother and let her know what's going on.

> *(**CHARLIE** exits into the house.)*

FLOSSIE. They's always sayin' that it ain't nutritional to feed your young-uns out of a can. Of course, ain't none of these people ever visited Crabapple Holler. Can goods was pretty much all the –

MAMIE. *(Interrupting.)* Flossie, would you please go on to the bathroom and stop holding us up?

> *(**FLOSSIE** sticks her tongue out at **MAMIE** and tings the hotel bell mischievously. She goes into the house. **DOWD** smiles privately.)*

*(To **DOWD**.)* What's got *you* so tickled?

DOWD. Flossie wanting to talk about cans and you sending her to the can.

> *(**MAMIE**, stone-faced, doesn't seem to see the humor. **ARPEGE** comes out. He is now dressed as a bell-boy, or more specifically a bell-girl, since he's still in makeup and wig.)*

ARPEGE. You rang?

MAYVONNE. We rang accidentally, Arpege.

> *(Looking around.)*

Unless anyone needs anything, now that he's here.

DOWD. I wouldn't mind a beer. I bet Charlie wouldn't either. Is there any beer in Trudy's fridge?

ARPEGE. *(Grinning.)* There's *always* beer in Trudy's fridge. Her maid just happens to like it that way.

MAMIE. Perhaps there might also be something stronger?

ARPEGE. We're pretty well-stocked, Ms. Ewing. Don't you remember all those parties Ms. Tromaine used to throw? We got everything from Old Lady sherry to industrial paint thinner.

MAMIE. Why don't you mix us up a nice pitcher of martinis? *(To the other women.)* If Arpege mixed us up a pitcher of martinis, would I be the only taker?

PATTY. I'd be a taker if it was an Appletini.

MAMIE. I don't know what that is, but I'm game.

ARPEGE. That's two beers. A pitcher of Appletinis. Any other special requests? Mayvonne?

> (**MAYVONNE** *shakes her head.* **ARPEGE** *starts to go.)*

PATTY. Arpege? Can you bring us some paper and pencils?

ARPEGE. Sure thing.

> *(He exits.)*

PATTY. *(To the others.)* It's probably a good idea – don't you think – to take our votes by secret ballot?

MAYVONNE. That *is* a good idea, Patty-cake. *(With snark.)* Perhaps we can put all of our *discussions* in writing, too.

VALERIE. I don't know what you think is going to happen here, Mayvonne. We're all friends.

MAYVONNE. Everyone's friends on the school board, but that doesn't stop people from trying to pry each other's heads off every month. And over the most picayune sorts of things. I had to go to these meetings because I was the teachers' representative, but it was something I always dreaded.

VALERIE. What kinds of things would they fuss about?

MAYVONNE. Here's something that haunts me to this day. Ten, eleven years ago, the principal of Hickman Hills High, Ms. Graham – do you remember Ms. Graham?

VALERIE. Was she the one with the *thing*?

> *(She points to a spot on her neck.)*

MAYVONNE. Yes. The *thing*. Yes, that was her. Anyway, Ms. Graham thought it might be a good idea to have a feminine napkin dispenser in the girls' restrooms like other high schools do, so the girls wouldn't always have to tramp all the way down to the nurse's office, should the need arise. I swear to you, Valerie, there were two board members – *male* board members – who actually raised a stink about it.

VALERIE. How do you raise a stink about something like that?

MAYVONNE. They said it "encouraged promiscuity."

VALERIE. Were these men missing-in-action the week they taught sex-ed in health class?

MAYVONNE. *(Chuckling with* **VALERIE.***)* Oh, Lord! The stories I could tell!

(**FLOSSIE** *and* **CORINNE** *come back out.*)

PATTY. *(To* **CORINNE.***)* Where's Charlie?

CORINNE. He's still on the phone.

MAMIE. Now, understanding this process: what we all have to decide is who will be the first person to be eliminated. Is that right, Patty?

PATTY. That's right.

FLOSSIE. *(Trying to understand.)* So when we vote *for* someone, we're actually votin' against 'em?

PATTY. Exactly.

MAYVONNE. Well, it all just sounds so *final*.

VALERIE. We aren't going to *kill* them, Mayvonne. We're just going to ask them to sit in the herb garden until we work our way down to the last person standing. And that will be the individual whose name we'll present to Trudy.

MAMIE. If no one minds, there's something I'd like to get out of the way, right here at the outset.

VALERIE. Uh-oh. Here we go.

MAMIE. Believe it or not, this isn't about *you*, Valerie. It just happens to be about Corinne.

(**CHARLIE** *now joins the others.*)

CORINNE. What about Corinne?

MAMIE. Well, it's probably more about your husband, I mean, when you get right down to it. You see, dear, I just don't think Dabney can be trusted. I mean, should you be the winner of this game.

CORINNE. Trusted to do *what*?

PATTY. To agree to divide the money fairly, I think Mamie means.

MAMIE. That's *exactly* what I mean. We all know the kind of influence he has over you, Corinne. And I, for one, am a little fearful that he might talk you into keeping all that money for yourselves.

CORINNE. But Dabney isn't like that at all! I also don't think you have very much respect for *me* – thinking I'd allow him to control me like that.

VALERIE. He's done it before, sugar. Not to mention: when it comes to money, Dabney's got a terrible track record. I remember when the two of you got married, your father wrote you a pretty big check as a wedding gift and did Dabney not take every penny of that money and go and invest it in something that didn't make a bit of sense?

MAMIE. (*Nodding.*) Invested it and lost it. Every cent of it.

DOWD. (*To* **CORINNE.**) What did he do with the money?

MAMIE. (*Not giving* **CORINNE** *a chance to answer.*) Put it into hairnets. Tell, him Corinne. Your husband put all that money from your father into men's hairnets.

DOWD. (*Trying to understand.*) There are men's hairnets that are different from women's hairnets? I thought hairnets were sort of, you know: *unisex.*

FLOSSIE. These had little bands of fabric around the bottom – didn't they, Corinne? – with little manly patterns like fighter jets and Conestoga wagons and kind of a camouflagey pattern, like if you was in the jungle, you and your hairnet could kinda blend in with the scenery.

CHARLIE. *(To* **DOWD.***)* Why would a man need a hairnet, anyway?

DOWD. Like if he was working in a restaurant kitchen or in a food plant or something. You don't want hair falling into your product.

FLOSSIE. I was eatin' a bag of Fritos one time and there was a tooth in there. I took it to Vincent and I said, "What kind of tooth is this, Vinnie Bear?" And he gave it a good look and said, "Why, honey, that looks to be a baby tooth. Some call it a milk tooth. I'm guessing a lateral incisor." "*Well,*" I said, "what's a baby's lateral incisor doin' in my bag of Frito corn chips?" "*Well,*" he said, "somebody must have brought their baby with them to the Frito-Lay assembly line one morning." You know: kind of like it was "Bring Your Baby to Work Day."

MAMIE. Flossie, I apologize for cutting you off, but what in the name of all that's holy does this have to do with Corinne's husband Dabney's inability to make sound financial decisions?

CORINNE. I swear to you – you really don't have to worry about him. If I got picked, I'd just tell him flat-out that it's *my* decision what happens to that money and he'll just have to respect that.

VALERIE. And has this "flat-out" approach ever worked with him before? Corinne, baby, this is all about trust and we don't trust that sneaky husband of yours any farther than we could throw him.

　　　(Turning to **PATTY.***)*

You've been friends with Corinne ever since she used to babysit for you. And you know Dabney better than most of us. Do you think Corinne could stand up to him if she had to?

PATTY. *(After considering the question for a moment; to* **CORINNE.***)* I know it's been very hard – the life you and Dabney have made together. And you can't hide the fact he's made some difficult demands on you.

CORINNE. He's looking for a job. I mean *seriously* looking. And I know he drinks, but he's stopped. He's stopped before, but this time I think he means to keep himself sober.

> (**ARPEGE** *enters with a tray of drinks [which also includes the requested paper and pencils].*)

ARPEGE. (*Oblivious to what is being discussed.*) Drinks, anyone?

> (*He sets the tray down on a table.*)

MAMIE. Thank you, Arpege. Now go away.

> (**ARPEGE,** *looking puzzled, goes back inside.* **CHARLIE,** *spying the paper and pencil, wordlessly distributes slips of paper and pencils among the G.G.s during the following exchange.*)

PATTY. Although, in Corinne's defense, something ought to be said for the fact that after eleven years, Corinne and Dabney are still together. It hasn't been easy, but they're still hanging in there.

CORINNE. Thank you, Patty. I do love him. Sometimes I think of him as a little boy – a lost little boy who can't find his way home.

MAMIE. Well, he certainly found his way to Valerie's bed about four years ago.

> (**VALERIE,** *who is in the process of pouring herself an Appletini from the pitcher, literally drops her glass on the floor.* **CORINNE** *crosses to* **MAMIE,** *gives her a look of both hurt and contempt, then leaves the porch to stand alone in the grass.* **PATTY** *watches her, then a moment later goes to join her. Through the dialogue that follows,* **PATTY** *will offer silent comfort.*)

VALERIE. (*Taking a moment to find her voice.*) Mamie Ewing, you promised me that you were going to take that confession of mine straight to the grave.

MAMIE. Well, I decided to take it to Trudy Tromaine's porch instead.

VALERIE. How *could* you?

MAMIE. How could I? We're about to make the biggest decision of our lives, and I just feel it would behoove us all to put *everything* on the table. Now, we all know that you have a bad habit of stepping out with other people's husbands and this just happens to make you – in my humble opinion – not the most responsible person on this porch. Any woman who would sleep with the spouse of one of her very own Glitter Girl sisters, could just as well steal sixteen million dollars from her friends and never look back.

DOWD. Technically, it would be *fourteen* million, since you'd assume that if it was divided evenly, two million would fairly be hers.

MAMIE. Dowd, with all due respect, could you please shut up?

MAYVONNE. *Mamie!*

VALERIE. *(To* **MAYVONNE.**) I'd slap her, but I might break my hand on that – that – oh, help me out, Mayvonne.

MAYVONNE. You mean Mamie's armor-like carapace of some reptilian origin? *This*, my fellow Glitter Girls, is what I *didn't* want to do. And now we're knee-deep in it. And I'm going to sit in the herb garden and sing hymns, in case any of you wishes to join me.

FLOSSIE. I would join you, Mayvonne, but that would mean I wouldn't get to vote. And I suddenly got me a very strong hankerin' to vote right now. So here's what we all got to decide: who do we kick off this here porch?

(Looking out at **CORINNE.**)

A Glitter Girl who dotes on her husband like he was the Goddang King of Sheba, when he ain't got the sense God gave a flea?

(Turning to **MAMIE.**)

A Glitter Girl who'd betray a secret just as quick as she'd swat a fly?

(Now turning to **VALERIE.***)*

Or a Glitter Girl with a bed that's racked up so much
rode-hard mileage, even the Goodwill wouldn't take it?
(To **MAYVONNE.***)* Now I'd say that's something definitely
worth sticking around for.

CHARLIE. *(Raising his hand like he was still in school.)*
Excuse me. *I'd* like to say something.

MAYVONNE. You go right ahead, honey.

(Always the teacher.)

But first get that hair out of your eyes.

CHARLIE. *(By habit.)* Yes, ma'am.

(He pulls the hair back from his forehead.)

[Note: if the actor playing **CHARLIE** *doesn't
have hair long enough to make this work,
feel free to substitute the line: "But stand
up straight, honey. Don't slouch." To which*
CHARLIE *will respond accordingly.]*

I'd just like to say something on behalf of one of those
women, if nobody minds.

VALERIE. Corinne was *your* babysitter too?

CHARLIE. *(To* **VALERIE.***)* It isn't about Corinne. It's about *you.*

VALERIE. *Me?*

CHARLIE. *(Nodding.)* It's about a special night we had when
I was fifteen.

(Selected gasps and eyebrow raises.)

MAMIE. Charlie Seaburn, you just better not be getting
ready to tell us that it was Valerie Fairhope who sent
you on your merry way to manhood.

CHARLIE. No, that isn't it at all. That would have been
statutory rape. Title sixteen of the Georgia Code,
chapter six, section three. No, what I'm saying is that I
was very shy at that age, and was really having a hard
time expressing myself around girls, and Valerie and I
had a long talk one night and she helped me sort a few
things out.

VALERIE. *(Touched.)* I *did*? I helped you that much?

CHARLIE. More than my mother ever –

> *(Catching himself.)*

I shouldn't talk about Mama that way, but I'm not supposed to have a filter, right? So I'll just say that it wasn't an easy thing going through adolescence with Barbara Seaburn at the rudder.

> **(PATTY** *now leads a recovering* **CORINNE** *back up onto the porch.)*

FLOSSIE. Do you hate your ma, Charlie? Is that *your* big flaw, sugar?

CHARLIE. I don't hate my mother. She can't help the way she is. But maybe we could say that about Valerie too. *And* Mamie. *And* Corinne.

PATTY. *(Re-entering the porch conversation.)* Charlie, that doesn't help us make our decision.

CHARLIE. I never said this was going to be a walk in the park. As a matter of fact, I just might decide not to vote against any of those three.

PATTY. Well, you have to vote against *somebody*, Charlie. That's the way this works.

CHARLIE. Maybe I'll just sit in the herb garden with Mayvonne and sing hymns.

MAYVONNE. As it so happens, honey, I just had a wee change of heart.

> *(She shoots daggers at* **MAMIE.**)

"The Old Rugged Cross" will have to wait. Shall we vote, class?

PATTY. *(Shrugging.)* I guess we vote.

> *(They put pencils to paper.* **PATTY** *tings the bell.)*

I think Arpege should be the tabulator. Does everyone agree?

> *(Nods and ad-libbed statements of agreement.* **ARPEGE** *comes out onto the porch.)*

FLOSSIE. We need you to count the votes, Girlboy.

ARPEGE. I can do that.

> *(As they finish, each hands his or her slip to* **ARPEGE.** *He sits down at a little table, and as he calls out the names that have been written on the paper slips he places them in little piles.)*

Okay.

> *(He takes a deep breath.)*

Mamie.

MAMIE. I'll bet that one came from Valerie. Does the paper smell of "Eau de Slut"?

FLOSSIE. Mamie, you hush up and let Arpege do her job.

ARPEGE. *Mamie.*

MAYVONNE. Another *Mamie.* My, oh my!

FLOSSIE. Everybody be *quiet*!

ARPEGE. *Corinne.*

> *(***CORINNE*** *winces.)*

Valerie. Another *Corinne.*

> *(***CORINNE*** *winces again.)*

Valerie.

MAMIE. That's two for you *too*, Valerie.

> *(***VALERIE*** *doesn't respond. She isn't taking her eyes off* **ARPEGE.***)*

ARPEGE. *Mamie.*

> *(***VALERIE*** *lets out a sigh of relief, then shoots* **MAMIE** *a look of goading triumph.)*

And last but not least: *Mayvonne.*

SEVERAL GLITTER GIRLS. *(Not* **MAYVONNE.***) Mayvonne?*

ARPEGE. That's what's written down here. You can see for yourself.

> *(He holds up the slip.)*

VALERIE. *(Taking the slip from* **ARPEGE.***)* Whose handwriting is this?

PATTY. It could be anybody. It's just capital letters.

FLOSSIE. Don't some teachers write only in capital letters? Mayvonne, honey, did you go and vote against yourself?

MAYVONNE. I absolutely did not. But now I'm very curious to know who *did* vote against me, and right off the bat.

> *(She eyes her companions but no one says anything.)*

CHARLIE. Excuse me, folks, but it is now our solemn duty to send someone to the herb garden. And that someone, by the official count is *you*, Mamie.

VALERIE. *(To* **MAMIE,** *in fun.)* I sure hope your husband does better in his mayor's race than you did here today: *loser*!

MAMIE. Well, I can't say I'm surprised. No matter how many nice things I did for all of you over all these years, it was never really enough, was it?

PATTY. It isn't that at all, Mamie. Somebody had to draw the first short straw and it just happened to be you. A change in just one vote and either Valerie or Corinne could have been the one going to the herb garden.

CHARLIE. *(To* **MAMIE.***)* Do you need help with your chair?

MAMIE. *(Bristling.)* I can carry my own chair, thank-you-very-much. So this doesn't mean I'm allowed to have anything else to say about this decision we're about to make?

FLOSSIE. To be fair, honey, you are now a persona something something. What is it, Mayvonne?

MAYVONNE. Mamie is persona non grata.
(To **MAMIE.***)* We'll tell you how it all turns out.

MAMIE. I'll have you all know that I have excellent hearing. I'm going to be listening to everything that's said up on this porch, so I'd advise you all to be very careful how you talk about me after I'm gone.

VALERIE. *(A la "Please Don't Talk About Me When I'm Gone.")*

"PLEASE DON'T TALK ABOUT HER WHILE SHE'S GONE!"

> *(She dissolves into laughter.* **MAMIE** *fumbles with her purse and the chair, and all watch in silence as she leaves the porch and crosses to the herb garden, where she promptly sets the chair down and herself in it, crosses her arms, and scowls.)*

PATTY. *(Privately to* **MAYVONNE**.*) You* cast one of those three votes against Mamie, didn't you?

MAYVONNE. *(Nodding, grinning mischievously.)* And it felt *so* good!

VALERIE. *(Going for the pitcher.)* I need a drink.

End of Act One

ACT TWO

(No time has passed since the end of Act One. Everyone is exactly where they were at the blackout/curtain: five GLITTER GIRLS and two MALE AUXILIARY MEMBERS on the porch, and MAMIE sitting alone in her wicker chair in the herb garden. Although none of this will be scripted, the characters will imbibe their various potent potables throughout the second act. This may contribute to heightened passions as the act goes along, but only one of the group – MAMIE – will become demonstrably inebriated. VALERIE goes to the edge of the porch and calls to her:)

VALERIE. Mamie, honey! You want me to bring you a drink?

MAMIE. *(Angry and refusing to even look at VALERIE.)* NO!

(Rethinks this.)

YES!

(To herself.) Since I'm in the herb garden I should probably drink something herbal.

(To VALERIE.) BRING ME A GIN RICKEY!

VALERIE. A what?

MAMIE. A. GIN. RICKEY.

VALERIE. Coming right up!

*(**VALERIE** goes to the table and taps the hotel bell.)*

CORINNE. *(To everyone.)* I'd like to say something.

FLOSSIE. You go right ahead and say something, sugar.

CORINNE. I wish to say that –

(Somehow finding the courage she needs to be uncharacteristically blunt.)

CORINNE. Well, I just can't believe that one of us actually voted against Mayvonne.

PATTY. Whoever it was must have had her reason.

(Her look taking in the two men.)

Or *his* reason.

VALERIE. *(An amused observation.)* Things were so much easier when there weren't men around.

*(To **DOWD** and **CHARLIE**, grinning mischievously.)* And we could all just talk behind your backs.

CORINNE. I'm just saying it would be nice to *know* that person's reason.

*(With a tender glance in **MAYVONNE**'s direction.)*

Mayvonne is probably the nicest and sweetest one of us all and I think it was just plain mean for somebody to do that.

VALERIE. Well, Mayvonne has said she didn't vote for herself and I'm fine telling all of you that *I* didn't vote for her. And Mamie pretty much let us all know that *she* was voting for *you*, Corinne. So the question becomes: which of the remaining four of you stuck your knife into poor, undeserving Mayvonne's back? Maybe *I'd* like to know that too.

MAYVONNE. *(To **VALERIE**.)* Well, *I* couldn't possibly care less, so why don't we just let it go?

*(**ARPEGE** steps out onto the porch.)*

ARPEGE. You rang?

VALERIE. Mamie wants a gin rickey. Do you know how to make a gin rickey?

ARPEGE. I was a bartender for eight years. I can make a dozen different *kinds* of rickeys. Even a "Little Rickey." It's like a banana daiquiri but without the rum.

(Lowering his voice, indicating **MAMIE**.*)* But is she allowed to drink? You just voted her off your island.

MAMIE. I HEARD THAT! I AM STILL A HUMAN BEING! *(To herself.)* A *thirsty* human being.

AND PUT IN *TWO* LIME HALVES. I LIKE MY RICKEYS VERY LIMEY.

(To herself.) Just like my first husband Nigel.

PATTY. *(To* **ARPEGE**.*)* Yes, Mamie can have a drink. Goodbye, Arpege.

*(***ARPEGE** *goes inside.)*

CORINNE. I hate to be a problem, but before we take another vote –

MAYVONNE. *(Interrupting.)* Really, honey – you don't have to come to my defense. Maybe somebody just didn't like the way I graded them when they were in my class.

FLOSSIE. That wouldn't include *me*. I went to one of them one-room schoolhouses where you got taught to the tune of a hickory stick.

VALERIE. What are you, Flossie? A hundred-and-thirty years old?

FLOSSIE. All's I'm *sayin'*, Val, is that I went to a country school – same as Trudy. So I didn't have Mayvonne for my teacher. I had Miss Lydia Beachy. She had a displaced hip, which made her whole body kind of list to the right. Sometimes she'd head over to the blackboard and end up just going around in a sad little circle.

DOWD. Corinne?

CORINNE. Yes?

DOWD. It was me. I was the one who voted against Mayvonne.

MAYVONNE. *You?*

(He nods.)

But why?

DOWD. Do I have to say? I thought maybe since we voted by secret ballot...

VALERIE. Well, you did just go and let the cat out of the bag, Dowd. You might as well tell us why the damned pussy was in there in the first place.

CORINNE. Was it like Mayvonne said, Dowd? Does it go back to when you were in the seventh grade?

DOWD. No, no. Mayvonne was actually one of my favorite teachers.

　　　(Beat.)

You know, I *really* don't like doing this.

　　　(He sits down and gets quiet.)

VALERIE. Well, all right then. I suppose some of our deep, dark secrets will just have to remain un-divulged.

DOWD. *(Turning around to face the others, his eyes now watering.)* It isn't the worst thing in the world. But I know that it hurt Mary Katherine.

MAYVONNE. Oh.

　　　(Beat.)

I think I know.

PATTY. Know what?

MAYVONNE. It's because I didn't go to see her after she got so sick. It's *that*, isn't it?

　　　*(**DOWD** nods.)*

FLOSSIE. Not at all?

　　　*(**MAYVONNE** shakes her head.)*

DOWD. Mayvonne was the only one of the Glitter Girls who never came. Not when Mary Katherine was in the hospital, not even later when I brought her home.

MAYVONNE. I didn't go to see her in the hospice either.

FLOSSIE. Did you never even call?

MAYVONNE. *(Helplessly, not defensively.)* I called her on Christmas.

DOWD. Yes. I remember Christmas. Mary Katherine was having a bad day and wasn't up to talking. The two of you were such good friends and I never understood it.

MAYVONNE. *(After a long pause, during which she gathers her thoughts.)* I didn't mean to be so cruel, Dowd. I was afraid. I was worried about feeling all those things I felt when I lost Jim. I lost him to cancer, too, Dowd, and it absolutely destroyed me. I just couldn't watch another person I loved slip away like that.

PATTY. *(To* **MAYVONNE.***)* I wonder, though, maybe if you'd made more of an effort – if you could have taken away something positive from just being there with her – something that might have actually helped you.

MAYVONNE. *(Not snidely, dabbing her own moist eyes.)* Was that something you learned in that bereavement group you went to after your mother passed?

VALERIE. *(Not giving* **PATTY** *a chance to answer.)* Grief's a bitch. Sometimes it drops you in a hole. Sometimes it makes you want to put your fist through the wall. I don't judge you, Mayvonne. But I don't judge Dowd either for being hurt by the choice you made.

MAYVONNE. *(Tears now forming in her eyes.)* Then y'all just go ahead and put me right over there in that herb garden with Mamie. Give me what I deserve. I wouldn't blame you in the least. I *did* take the easy way out. I'm so sorry, Dowd. I'm so sorry I ran away.

> *(***MAYVONNE*** extends a hand toward* **DOWD**.
> *He hesitates, but finally takes it.)*

FLOSSIE. *(To* **MAYVONNE.***)* Well, I don't see you runnin' away from Trudy. You're right here with all the rest of us. And this whole thing ain't easy. And I'm not just talkin' about Trudy dying. I'm referrin' to this nasty thing she's makin' us all do *before* she dies.

> *(***ARPEGE*** steps out with* **MAMIE**'s *gin rickey
> and crosses down to the herb garden.)*

CHARLIE. Do we keep talking or do we take another vote?

CORINNE. I'm ready to take another vote.

> (**CORINNE** *musters a smile for* **MAYVONNE,** *who is unable to do the same.* **CHARLIE** *passes out another round of makeshift ballots. Everyone goes to separate chairs and corners to think and then to vote. Meanwhile, in the herb garden:)*

MAMIE. *(Taking the drink from* **ARPEGE**.*)* Thank you, sir. *Or ma'am.* Do I have to tip you?

ARPEGE. Of course you don't have to tip me.

MAMIE. Well, anyway: *thank you.* And thank you for the two lime halves. You know: you remind me of someone. I just can't put my finger on it.

ARPEGE. Everybody's always saying I look like somebody or another. Which is kind of weird to hear because...

> *(Makes a self-indicating gesture.)*

...hello!

MAMIE. I find your look sort of unsettling. You look like a creepy department store mannequin.

ARPEGE. *(With a hint of sarcasm.)* Um. *Thank you?*

> *(He starts back up to the porch.)*

CHARLIE. *(To his companions on the porch.)* Everybody done?

> *(Nods and ad-libbed "yes's." **CHARLIE** collects the slips of paper. **ARPEGE** takes his seat at what has now become the tabulation table. Everyone gathers around. **MAMIE** even gets up out of her chair and stands near the porch to look on.)*

ARPEGE. Okay.

> *(He begins, calling out names as he goes through the slips of paper.)*

Valerie.

VALERIE. Cheeze! What am I? The flavor of the damned month?

(**FLOSSIE** *"shushes" her with a flutter of the hand.*)

ARPEGE. *Mayvonne. Valerie.*

(**VALERIE** *groans.*)

Patty.

VALERIE. *Patty?*

FLOSSIE. Valerie, if you don't close that big hotdog mouth of yours, I'm gonna close it for you.

VALERIE. But who could possibly vote against Patty? The only one of us who didn't want her as a legacy G.G. is sitting over there making love to her tonic and gin.

MAMIE. I'm not in the herb garden, Val. I'm standing right here, listening to every dirty little word you're saying.

VALERIE. Well, why don't you go back to all that smelly fennel and dill, and leave us the hell alone?

MAMIE. Don't you worry, my pretty. I predict that you'll be joining me very, very soon!

PATTY. *(Stepping completely out of character.)* Will the two of you please kindly *shut up*? Arpege is trying to count the votes and I'm curious to know if anyone *else* has suddenly decided that I'm a danger to society.

(**PATTY** *appears distraught.* **CHARLIE** *moves to comfort her but she is too worked-up to notice his overture.*)

ARPEGE. Um. Where were we?

DOWD. It was *Valerie*: two. *Mayvonne* and *Patty*: one each.

ARPEGE. And we have a *Corinne*. And we have another *Mayvonne*. And last but not least – well, maybe in this case, "least" *would* be the right word: a third *Mayvonne*.

FLOSSIE. *(To* **VALERIE**, *tauntingly.)* You're gettin' pretty good at dodgin' them bullets, ain't you, shug?

PATTY. *(To* **MAYVONNE**.*)* You actually *did* vote for yourself this time, didn't you?

(**MAYVONNE** *nods.*)

PATTY. And yet I can't think of a better person for making sure that money got fairly distributed than you.

MAYVONNE. And how do you know that, sweetie? How do we know anything about anybody? It's a real afternoon of surprises, honey. And most of them aren't very *good* surprises. So I'll be content just to sit among all the smelly fennel and dill until this horrible, no-good afternoon is finally over.

(**PATTY** *taps the bell.*)

ARPEGE. *(To* **PATTY**.*)* I'm right here, love.

PATTY. I'm sorry, Arpege. I didn't see you.

ARPEGE. Yes, this bright red uniform of mine does tend to blend in, don't it?

PATTY. I want a gin rickey.

VALERIE. I thought you were drinking Appletinis.

PATTY. I was. And now I want a gin rickey.

(**ARPEGE** *goes inside as* **MAYVONNE** *makes her way off the porch and crosses to the herb garden.*)

(To her porch companions, importantly.) Okay. Fess up. Which one of you bitches voted against me?

CORINNE. *(Shocked.) Patty!*

VALERIE. *(Amused; overlapping* **CORINNE**.*)* Get a hold of yourself, girl!

CHARLIE. *(Minimizing.)* It was just the one person, Patty.

PATTY. That's what makes it hurt so much. That there's one of you who stands alone against me. When I thought everybody *liked me*!

FLOSSIE. Maybe it ain't that at all, sweet pea. Maybe it's got nothin' at all to do with not liking you.

PATTY. *(Suddenly suspicious.)* You said that like you knew what you were talking about.

FLOSSIE. *(Uneasily.)* I'm just sayin' –

(All eyes are now on **FLOSSIE**.*)*

Why are y'all all lookin' at me like that?

PATTY. I don't know, Flossie. I'd been thinking it was probably Corinne.

CORINNE. *Me?*

PATTY. Because of all those things Petey and I used to do to you when you were our babysitter. Like that time we tied you to a chair and then ran off to get Icee slushes at the Handy Mandy. You just laughed it off at the time. Yet it left deep scars, didn't it?

DOWD. *(Before* **CORINNE** *can respond, to* **PATTY**.*)* You have a brother named Petey?

PATTY. *Peter.* He's my younger brother. When we were kids we all called him Petey.

DOWD. "Petey and Patty." That's fun.

(He smiles.)

My brother's name was Vernon. But because he had a voice like a foghorn, we gave him the nickname "Loud." As boys, we were "Dowd and Loud."

FLOSSIE. *(Unsmiling.)* That's real funny, Dowd. Now I'm gonna tell you why I voted for Patty and then we're all gonna just hush up about it.

(Takes a moment to let this disclosure settle in, then to **PATTY***:)*

You remember that nephew of mine from the hills that came down to live with Vincent and me? Jubal. Jubal Lee. Vincent worked on his teeth. Jubal had really bad teeth. Most hill people do. But then after all that was done he stayed on so he could get his diploma from Hickman High. Over time, why, Vincent and me – we just started to feel like Jubal was our very own son. We couldn't have no biological children, don't-cha-know, on account of Vincent's sperm. Well, they got no tails.

PATTY. I remember Jubal. He ran track with Charlie.

CHARLIE. He liked the hurdles.

FLOSSIE. He also liked Patty. Liked her quite a bit, as I recall. *(To* **PATTY**.*)* He asked you to go to the junior prom with him, now didn't he?

PATTY. *(Dodging.)* Did he? I don't remember.

FLOSSIE. You don't remember? *He* remembered. It broke his heart when you said no. He was never the same again.

PATTY. Oh, Flossie, that's not fair. A bunch of boys asked me. I ended up going with Warren Wilburn.

FLOSSIE. And my nephew ended up going to the Georgia State Prison for armed robbery.

VALERIE. Flossie Price! Are you saying that just because Patty turned Jubal down for the junior prom – this launched him into a life of crime?

FLOSSIE. As far as I could tell, he was a real good boy until that happened.

PATTY. Flossie, can I be honest?

     (FLOSSIE *nods.)*

He had really bad dandruff. And he smelled like scalp. He smelled like he never ever washed his hair. I'd walk into a classroom and the whole room would have that scalpy smell, and I'd think, "Well, Jubal's got to be in here somewhere, because the whole room smells like scalp, and there he'd be, wearing that white-speckled ski cap that used to be brown, and I'd have to find me a desk by the windows so I could breathe.

FLOSSIE. He may not have washed his hair as often as he oughta have, but I'll have you know that he did give that head of his a real good scrubbing the night of the prom. But that didn't make no never mind; you thought you was too good for him.

PATTY. *(Exasperated.)* Flossie, I just *told you* –!

DOWD. Flossie, I don't quite understand how Patty's decision not to go to the prom with a boy who had hygiene issues should have anything to do with whether Patty could be a good custodian of that inheritance money.

FLOSSIE. It's just somethin' I never got past. The same way you never got past Mayvonne not comin' to see Mary Katherine.

(This seems to hurt **DOWD***, but he doesn't respond.)*

PATTY. *(To* **FLOSSIE***.)* Would it help if I said I was sorry? I was sixteen. All these boys were asking me to the prom and it was a little overwhelming.

CHARLIE. *I* didn't ask you. I wanted to, but I just couldn't get up the nerve. I went stag and stood against the wall with all the other guys who didn't have dates. At one point, Jubal Lee and I went out and snuck a smoke together. And I can attest to the fact that he actually *did* wash his hair that night. It was very fragrant. It smelled like gardenias.

FLOSSIE. That was the conditioner.

CHARLIE. Is there anything that anyone else wants to say or should I get Arpege so we can take another vote?

PATTY. I'd like to say something else if nobody minds. It's about Corinne. Corinne, you need to tell everybody that Petey and I didn't tie that rope very tight and you could have wiggled out of it if you'd wanted to, but you were having too much fun. I don't want everybody to think I was both a terrible teenager *and* a terrible child.

CORINNE. Oh, I know it was mostly Petey who came up with all the pranks, Patty.

MAYVONNE. I don't recall ever having had Peter as a student.

PATTY. That's because my parents sent him to military school. When he grew up he became an eco-terrorist. He sends me Christmas cards made out of elephant dung paper.

CHARLIE. *(Not sarcastic.)* That was – okay, that was interesting, Patty.

(He taps the bell and begins to hand out the slips of paper. **ARPEGE** *comes out and takes his place at the table. Everyone votes. Meanwhile, in the herb garden:)*

MAMIE. *(To* **MAYVONNE***.)* I know things about everyone on that porch. Things that I don't think anyone else knows. But I don't get to be useful. I have to sit here like a knot on a log.

MAYVONNE. *(To* **MAMIE.***)* Maybe there are some things that just shouldn't be said.

MAMIE. I thought the idea was to get everything out in the open.

MAYVONNE. Was that the idea, Mamie? If that was the idea, it's a cocka*mamie* one.

MAMIE. Why, Mayvonne Rausch, you made a funny!

> *(Everyone passes his or her slips to* **ARPEGE***. He takes a deep breath.)*

ARPEGE. *Flossie.*

> *(Next slip:)*

Patty.

> *(Next slip:)*

Corinne.

> *(Next slip:)*

Corinne.

> *(Next slip:)*

Another Corinne.

> *(Last slip:)*

And *Valerie.*

CORINNE. *(Taking it in stride.)* Well, okay.

CHARLIE. It's nothing personal, Corinne. I'm still just a little nervous about Dabney and his influence over you.

CORINNE. Well, it's nothing personal, Charlie, but if your mother had been here instead of you, I would have voted against *her*, so I guess that makes things even.
(To **ARPEGE***.)* Am I supposed to ask for a gin rickey before you send me to the Island of Misfit Toys?

MAMIE. *(Calling to* **CORINNE***.)* CORINNE, YOU MADE A FUNNY!

CHARLIE. *(To* **CORINNE.***)* Would you mind telling me why you would have voted against my mother?

CORINNE. Well, I *do* mind, but since I happened to bring it up, you should know that it's because of your mother that Dabney got his driver's license suspended for a year. For a whole year I had to drive him to and from work – that was back when he still had a job – and it was a terrible inconvenience because of how far away it was.

CHARLIE. Why would my mother have anything to do with that? She isn't a traffic court judge.

CORINNE. After he got picked up on that DUI, he and I went to her and asked her to represent him. I thought that since she was a Glitter Girl and *I* was a Glitter Girl, she'd do us this favor. She said no.

CHARLIE. She must have had a good reason.

CORINNE. Your mother's reason was that she didn't believe Dabney when he said he hadn't been drinking. But he *hadn't* been drinking! He'd just breathed in a little too much of that patio sealant he was using to repair our back deck, and he probably should have waited a while before he went to pick up our girls from soccer. Your mother could have gotten him off based on the fact that he wasn't aware that a person shouldn't fix a patio and then get right into their car. But she turned her back on us. And Dabney had to go to one of those lawyers that advertised on cable TV in the middle of the night. And that was like not going to anybody at all.

(To **ARPEGE.***)* I *will* have a gin rickey. But put in more gin than rickey, if you please.

> *(As* **ARPEGE** *exits into the house,* **CORINNE** *picks up her chair, leaves the porch, and crosses to the herb garden.)*

VALERIE. Corinne made a good point, and probably didn't even realize it: Mary Katherine and Barbara Seaburn shouldn't get off the hook just because they aren't here.

DOWD. I'd like to know what Mary Katherine could possibly have done that would put her in everybody's crosshairs.

VALERIE. I'm just speaking in general terms, Dowd.

CHARLIE. *(Reeling.)* No, what you're doing is speaking in *specific* terms, and specifically about my mother. Not that it's an easy thing to defend her.

> *(Beat.)*

So I'm not *going* to defend her.

VALERIE. Don't we all agree that Barbara Seaburn just might not be the best person to make sure we all got a fair portion of that money?

CHARLIE. And why is that?

VALERIE. Well. She's a lawyer. I rest my case.

CHARLIE. I still don't understand why that would disqualify her from doing the right thing.

VALERIE. What do you throw to a drowning lawyer?

CHARLIE. *What?*

VALERIE. *(It's a riddle.)* What do you throw to a drowning lawyer? His partners. Why won't sharks attack lawyers? Professional courtesy. What do dinosaurs and decent lawyers have in common? They're both extinct.

CHARLIE. Are you going to quote the whole joke book?

VALERIE. I just might.

PATTY. Valerie, you do know that Charlie's in law school right now, right?

VALERIE. *(To CHARLIE.)* My condolences.

FLOSSIE. I think it's time to send our hateful friend Valerie to the herb garden. I'll tell you whatever you need to know about her. She's got a big trunk full of secrets and I have the key.

VALERIE. Everybody knows I used to be a pole dancer. Everybody knows I used to sleep around.

FLOSSIE. But do they know who you slept *with*? I mean, in addition to Corinne's husband Dabney?

VALERIE. Weren't you just a little while ago beating up on Mamie for spilling the beans about Dabney and me?

FLOSSIE. Well, this here is a different ballgame now, Val, honey. We got only five of us left on this porch, and I already got myself in trouble with Patty. Well, truth be told, darlin', if I told everything I knew about you, they wouldn't be able to kick you off this porch fast enough.

DOWD. *I* wouldn't.

FLOSSIE. Well, of course you wouldn't. You had no problem goin' to Valerie for some lovin' while your wife was sick.

> (*Momentary silence as this statement gets communally digested.*)

DOWD. It isn't what you think.

VALERIE. Flossie: why are you doing this?

PATTY. Trudy did this. Trudy did this to all of us. I wish I'd never gotten out of bed this morning.

> (**PATTY** *drops into a chair, gloomy and defeated.*)

DOWD. Mary Katherine came to me. She said she felt sorry for me because we couldn't be intimate the way we were before she got sick. She knew I'd always had a little crush on Valerie. Hell, all the Glitter Girl husbands did. So she set it up for Valerie and me to be together.

PATTY. That sounds like something out of a movie.

DOWD. It was just my wife's way – I know it was weird, I know that some of you could never understand it – but it was her special way of showing how much she loved me.

> (*Beat.*)

She also collected vintage Barbie dolls and ceramic pigs. (*With husbandly pride.*) Mary Katherine was one of a kind.

VALERIE. And it ended up just being that one night. Neither of us wanted it to continue.

> (**DOWD** *confirms this with a nod.*)

FLOSSIE. (*To* **VALERIE,** *with sarcastic bite.*) Well, don't that make *you* "Slut of the Year"?

PATTY. Flossie, I'm not sure why you're turning on Valerie like this. I'm pretty sure she didn't share this with you just so you could use it against her later.

FLOSSIE. I'm not turning on Valerie. I'm not turning on any of you. It's you who already done turned on *me*. A long time ago. When I realized ain't none of you was ever gonna use my husband as your personal family dentist. Not a single one of you.

MAMIE. *(Injecting her opinion from across the yard.)* WHY SHOULD DEAN AND I GO TO VINCENT PRICE? WE ALREADY HAD A DENTIST! WE LIKED HIM *JUST FINE*!

PATTY. *(To* **FLOSSIE.***)* You want the truth? The reason I didn't go to your husband was because I was afraid of him. Not because his name was Vincent Price. It's because I'd heard the stories about people's crowns falling out and their bridges not holding. And sometimes your husband would accidentally drill the wrong tooth. I heard about that happening from two different people. Don't look at me that way, Flossie. I'm just telling you what people told *me*. And you know that whitening treatment he used – the one that made a person look like they had – what was it my mother used to call it? – *Jesus teeth*. Teeth that glowed, and not in a good way – like they were *electric*. Who wants electric Jesus teeth, Flossie?

FLOSSIE. I'll admit that Vincent isn't the dentist he used to be.

VALERIE. Flossie, sugar, I don't think Vincent's *ever* been the dentist he used to be.

MAMIE. VALERIE MADE A YOGI! HOME RUN, VALERIE!

FLOSSIE. I've been after him to retire. Ever since he got the dementia.

PATTY. So can you blame people for not wanting to go to him?

FLOSSIE. *(Beaten down.)* No, ma'am. I can't blame people for nothin'.

> *(She taps the bell to summon* **ARPEGE***. Apparently he was just inside the door and immediately steps out.)*

VALERIE. Have you been eavesdropping?

> *(***CHARLIE*** holds up what will quickly be revealed to be a small microphone, which he's pulled out from the cushion of a chair.)*

CHARLIE. Apparently, Arpege isn't the *only* one.

> *(Everyone gathers around to inspect the miniature listening device.)*

What does this look like to you, Arpege?

ARPEGE. *(Looking at it closely.)* A dead roach?

DOWD. That's a bug all right, but not the insect kind.

PATTY. Arpege, is she up there listening to us?

ARPEGE. *(Reluctantly.)* Yes.

FLOSSIE. How come?

ARPEGE. You don't think she has an interest in how the game turns out?

VALERIE. But wouldn't that interest be served by just finding out who we picked? This is something more.

ARPEGE. I'm not at liberty to say what more it is.

VALERIE. *(Sotto voce.)* Pass out the paper, Charlie. Don't make her mad. We have to play the game or else we might lose everything.

ARPEGE. Now you're talking. Move along, folks. Nothing to see here!

> *(In the herb garden* **MAMIE** *now jumps to her feet, seized by an epiphany.)*

MAMIE. *(To* **ARPEGE***.)* I know who you are now!

> *(She races over to the porch stairs.)*

FLOSSIE. You cain't come up on this porch, Mamie. You're banished.

MAMIE. I'll damned well come up on this porch if I damned well want to.

(To **ARPEGE.***)* I know now why your face has been on the tip of my tongue. You're the one who stole all that money from my husband's insurance company. I remember the pictures from the security cameras. I remember those eyes. *Your* eyes. They never caught the person.

VALERIE. They never caught the person because he either left town or went into hiding.

(Indicating **ARPEGE***'s female disguise.)*

I suppose a thief could hide just as well this way as any other.

MAMIE. I don't think he's hiding very well at all. Because I just caught him!

PATTY. Mamie, can we deal with your miraculous discovery later? I also notice that you're very drunk.

ARPEGE. That's fine by me. And if it *was* me, maybe I had my reasons.

MAYVONNE. *(To no one in particular.)* Just a minute ago, Mamie called me *Bethel*. I'm not sure Bethel's even a person's name.

VALERIE. Mayvonne and Corinne, can you escort the very drunk Mamie Ewing back to the garden?

MAMIE. I'll have you all know that I'm *sone stober*!

VALERIE. I'd imagine her husband's campaign people wouldn't want it getting out to the voting public that Dean Ewing is married to *that*.

MAMIE. *(Taking additional umbrage.)* Oh, so now I'm reduced to a relative pronoun!

> (**MAYVONNE** *and* **CORINNE***, flanking an unsteady* **MAMIE***, take her back to the herb garden.* **CHARLIE** *passes out the slips of paper, which everyone scribbles on and*

then immediately hands to **ARPEGE**. *They're getting very good at this.* **ARPEGE** *sits down.)*

ARPEGE. Do you all trust me to do this, or do you think I'll abscond with these slips while giving you all the stink-eye?

(He glances over at **MAMIE**, *in reference to her accusation that continues to hang in the air.)*

FLOSSIE. We trust you, Arpege. Deliver the goods, honey.

ARPEGE. *(Looking over the slips.)* Well, this one's easy. Four *Flossies* and one *Patty*.

PATTY. If Flossie didn't vote for herself, I have a very good idea who voted for *me*.

FLOSSIE. Well, all I can say is I'm glad to be out of it. And I don't want no gin rickey. I want a Jim Beam. Neat. *(To* **ARPEGE**.) Did you hear what I said, *thief*?

ARPEGE. Is this what we're doing now? We're all going to be taking our potshots at ol' Arpege?

FLOSSIE. You ain't the only one, sweetie.

(She crosses over to **CHARLIE** *and talks into the listening device he still holds in his hand.)*

I hope you're enjoying all this, you wizened, dyin' old hillbilly woman. And I'm sick of your uppityness and your pridefulness, and all this pretendin' you don't know where you came from! I'll tell you where you came from: the poorest, lowliest holler in the whole county. You and your no-count trash family brought down property values all over the goddang mountain!

PATTY. Do you really want Trudy on your bad side, Flossie?

FLOSSIE. Didn't you notice all them pieces of paper? I got *ever-body* on my bad side, looks like. And I got a husband who shouldn't be rootin' around in people's mouths no more on account of he ain't got himself enough bricks in his hod, and I got worn-out lungs that get me winded on the stairs and a damned womb that couldn't never sprout a child, and what child I did get as a consolation prize – the adopted one – ain't up for parole for another four years. I tell you my life is pretty much in the portapotty, folks, so do I care to tick off a woman who has done a pretty good job of showin' us she's got a mean streak about a mile wide? I could not possibly care less!

(*To* **ARPEGE**.) Bring me a glass of that Seven Year, if you got it. If you don't, I'll take the Devil's Cut. If you don't got either, bring me a damned Jack Daniels.

VALERIE. I thought you and Vincent were Southern Baptists.

FLOSSIE. Only on Sunday mornin's and Wednesday nights.

> (*She steps off the porch and joins* **MAMIE**, **MAYVONNE**, *and* **CORINNE** *in the herb garden as* **ARPEGE** *goes inside.*)

CHARLIE. (*To* **PATTY**.) I *wanted* to ask you to the prom. I really did. I was just so shy back in those days. I also had that terrible acne problem. Maybe you liked my neck so much because it was the only place on my body that didn't have zits.

PATTY. It's okay that you didn't ask me to the prom.

> (*Beat, then with a smile:*)

But I wish you had.

CHARLIE. (*Brightening.*) Are you saying you would have said yes?

PATTY. (*Nodding.*) Six different boys asked me. And I still would have picked you.

CHARLIE. (*Beaming.*) Well, who would have thought it?

PATTY. And *I'm* not one of those people who put down lawyers. It's been lawyers who've been on the front lines of all of our country's most important social struggles.

CHARLIE. And I think you going into social work is a pretty admirable thing, too. I know that social workers work really hard and never get paid enough for all the good things they do.

PATTY. Thank you, Charlie.

CHARLIE. I killed my father.

PATTY. What?

CHARLIE. I killed my father.

> *(Long beat.)*

I didn't mean to. It was an accident. He fell down the basement stairs. But I was the one responsible. I left one of my toy trucks at the top of the steps.

> *(**ARPEGE** comes out with **FLOSSIE**'s drink. He doesn't serve it to her in the garden, though, because **FLOSSIE** and her three companions are now making their way across the lawn to better hear **CHARLIE**'s confession.)*

VALERIE. Barbara never said anything about your father stepping on a toy truck. She just said it was dark and he missed a stair.

CHARLIE. The truth is that he stepped on the Tonka truck that I'd left there. I was six. I killed my father. That's *my* big, horrible secret.

MAYVONNE. *(To **CHARLIE**.)* Nobody could ever blame you for something like that.

> *(The two groups come together around the edge of the porch and for the next couple of minutes the gap between them is bridged.)*

CHARLIE. I blame myself, though. Maybe that's why I've always had – you know: *issues.*

PATTY. *(Sympathetic.)* If it makes you feel any better, I'm just fine with your *issues.* In fact, I wouldn't have you any other way.

CHARLIE. Wait a minute. Are you *having* me?

PATTY. I just mean: I like you the way you are.

CHARLIE. You *like* me?

PATTY. I like you. Maybe we could change the subject.

CHARLIE. Can we change the subject to the fact that I like *you* too?

PATTY. *(Blissfully.)* I like that topic even more.

> *(**CHARLIE** smiles.)*

PATTY. *(To the others on the porch.)* I have an idea. Why don't we stop all this voting, and those of us who are still left in this competition can just talk this out until we come to a mutual decision?

MAYVONNE. Any chance the four of us in the grass could join the four of you up there on the porch?

VALERIE. I have a better idea: why don't the four of us up here on the porch join you four snakes in the grass?

DOWD. That sounds like a plan. I was starting to feel like I might be spending the rest of my life on this porch.

ARPEGE. Are you sure you don't all want to stay up here with all the bacon puffs and caviar?

CHARLIE. No, I believe the consensus is that we all move to the yard, where we can speak freely...if you get my drift.

(He gives the listening device to **ARPEGE**.*)*

ARPEGE. I'm sorry about your dad.

CHARLIE. Thanks.

(The four game survivors pick up their chairs from the porch, those who had been in the herb garden get theirs, and everyone converges elsewhere in the yard. In the process, **MAMIE** *has an opportunity to speak with* **ARPEGE**.*)*

MAMIE. It *was* you, wasn't it? You say you "might have had your reasons." I just have to know. We've been wondering for years how someone could just walk into an insurance company, stick it up, and then just disappear into thin air.

ARPEGE. And I've always wondered how somebody could miss paying the premium on their parents' homeowner's policy by a matter of only a few lousy hours and then watch them lose everything when the house goes up in flames before he can get in with the check. I was wrong to put off making that payment until the next day but in my own defense, I did call to let your husband know. Trouble was, I couldn't understand a thing his secretary was saying on the phone, and so I hung up in frustration.

MAMIE. *(Nodding.)* Dean was always telling Rosebelle: "Don't answer the phone! Don't answer the phone!" She never listened. Rosebelle has no tongue. I always thought it was congenital, but Dean hinted at something having to do with a frozen flagpole when she was a girl. In any event, my husband felt terrible about your family's case. It's the worst-case scenario, isn't it?

MAYVONNE. *(Overhearing.)* So many difficult challenges for so many of us – each of us beat up and beat down in some way. Trudy doesn't understand this. Trudy doesn't understand that just because she was able to do all those nice things for us, that still didn't mean that life was ever a bowl of cherries – not for any of us.

> *(**ARPEGE** considers the mini-mike in his hand and then slings it across the yard.)*

ARPEGE. I've made a decision. I'm ready to be Arnold again. Mamie, will you let me be Arnold again without having to do jail time?

MAMIE. That isn't up to me, Arp–
(Correcting herself.) Arnold. But I do have a lot of sway with my husband. I'll see what I can do.

CHARLIE. *(To* **ARPEGE**.*)* I'll be happy to pitch in if you need an almost-lawyer on your side.

ARPEGE. *(Smiling warmly.)* Thank you: both of you.

> *(He takes off the hat and the wig, wipes away the lipstick with a handkerchief, and lets* **ARNOLD CROSS** *emerge.)*

VALERIE. So. Who's getting the money?

> *(Indicating herself.)*

The town tramp?

> *(Indicating* **CHARLIE**.*)*

A future lawyer with major self-esteem issues?

> *(Indicating* **PATTY**.*)*

Someone responsible for a man's life of crime?

PATTY. *(Protesting.) That's not fair!*

FLOSSIE. (*Privately to* **PATTY.**) Jubal asks about you. All this time. He wants to know if you still smell like honeysuckle and mountain rain.

VALERIE. Or do we turn all that money over to Mary Katherine's loving husband Dowd Foster –

FLOSSIE. Who was always trying to get Vincent to buy new tires sooner than he needed them?

MAMIE. (*To* **FLOSSIE.**) Did that happen to you too? And Dean could have sworn they scattered nails and razor-sharp shavings of sheet metal up and down Montgomery Road near the store. He always imagined people thumpety-thumping into the tire store parking lot, considering themselves lucky that their blow-outs happened so close to a *lo-and-behold* tire store.

DOWD. If I'd ever found out that my employees were pulling stuff like that I would've fired them on the spot!

(*Beat; then with questionable sincerity:*)

If, you know, I'd ever found out.

MAYVONNE. I suppose that for the four of you who still have a vote in this – if we were to use the metric of "Who has yet to get themselves a vote of no-confidence?" well, then, it would logically come down to either Charlie or Dowd. On the other hand, picking either Charlie or Dowd seems odd since they're the only two people here who –

VALERIE. (*Finishing* **MAYVONNE**'s *sentence.*) Don't have bazongas?

(*She cups her own breasts to make her point.*)

MAYVONNE. (*Snippily.*) I was *going* to say: ...Who isn't a *Glitter Girl.*

PATTY. Excuse me, Mayvonne, but Charlie is here for his mother – a Glitter Girl – and Dowd is here in memory of his wife – also a Glitter Girl.

MAMIE. I for one couldn't care less if the money is filtered through one of our male auxiliary members. Just so long as it isn't Dowd.

CORINNE. What?

VALERIE. Yeah. What's *this* all about?

MAMIE. I just found out a couple of days ago that our friend here gave a very large campaign contribution to one of my husband's mayoral opponents.

DOWD. There's no law that says I can't support whoever I want to.

MAMIE. And yet one husband of a Glitter Girl not supporting another husband of a Glitter Girl – it just smacks of: *so wrong.*

DOWD. But Mamie, I'm not even a Republican!

MAMIE. Still it rankles.

VALERIE. Since only Patty and Dowd and Charlie and me still have a vote, what you care about or *don't* care about, Mamie, doesn't matter one whit.

CHARLIE. Patty's right, though. It wouldn't really be a *man* you'd be voting for if you picked me. It would actually be my mother. *She's* the Glitter Girl. I'm just her stand-in.

MAMIE. And just where – I wonder – is all that money going to wind up? Probably some Cayman Island bank account, no doubt.

CHARLIE. *(To MAMIE.)* You really think that about my mother?

VALERIE. What's the difference between a mosquito and a lawyer?

MAYVONNE. Valerie, honey, *please*!

PATTY. On the other hand, Mary Katherine isn't here to speak for herself and yes, it might be a nice gesture to put the money in Dowd's hands in her honor, but I'm more inclined to go with Charlie.

> *(She smiles with romantic affection at* **CHARLIE.** *He smiles back, obviously equally enamored.)*

VALERIE. Would you like me to get you two a room? Cheeze!

PATTY. You think the only reason I want to vote for Charlie is because I *like* him?

FLOSSIE. We do, baby child. We do.

VALERIE. Well, this whole thing is getting too silly. I'll go with Charlie just to get this over with.

CHARLIE. And I'll make it easy on everybody and vote for myself.

DOWD. Which makes three. Charlie: you get the money. Or rather, your mother gets the money. I'm with Valerie; I'm just glad this thing is finally over.

CHARLIE. I should call Mama. She asked me to let her know how everything turned out.

> *(He steps away from the others, turns his back, and makes the call to his mother.)*

MAMIE. Arnold Cross, you go tell that rich lady you work for that our game has come to an end. We've made our pick.

> *(**ARNOLD** starts toward the porch just as **TRUDY** steps out. She is wearing a smart tennis outfit and appears the picture of health. She bounds down the stairs into the backyard, leaving those assembled in a state of complete shock and awe.)*

FLOSSIE. *(To **TRUDY**.)* Why on earth are you dressed like that?

TRUDY. I have a tennis date at six.

MAYVONNE. But you're supposed to be dying.

TRUDY. We'll I'm not.

FLOSSIE. But you have an inverted spleen –!

TRUDY. My spleen is just fine, Flossie. That was just my pretext for getting you all together.

VALERIE. So all of this –

TRUDY. It was an experiment, honey lambs.

MAMIE. So you're *not* giving away sixteen million dollars?

TRUDY. Oh, I'm still giving away the money.

(Thumb-pointing at **CHARLIE**.*)* Is that the lucky winner? I was having a hard time picking up the last ten minutes of your discussion.

PATTY. *(Nodding.)* It's Charlie.

(Correcting herself.) Well, his *mother*.

MAMIE. *(To* **TRUDY**.*)* So you really do intend to keep your promise about leaving all that money after you die?

TRUDY. Oh Mamie, I plan to do much better than that. By my calculation, Barbara Seaburn will have all those millions in hand in about five to six weeks. It was always my intention to give that money to the winner as soon as I possibly could.

(Calling over to **CHARLIE**.*)* Did you get that, Charlie?

> *(He nods. A cloud has now settled over* **CHARLIE***'s face. Something he is hearing from his mother seems to be responsible for this. At present, though, no one seems to be registering this fact.)*

Where's Arpege?

> *(***ARNOLD** *raises his hand.)*

Good God! *You* aren't Arpege!

ARNOLD. Arpege is gone, Ms. Tromaine. And she isn't coming back.

TRUDY. Oh. Well. I suppose I'll need some time to process this.

ARNOLD. Would you like me to *help* you process this?

TRUDY. *(Smiling.)* Tonight? Over *Vin Santo* and almond biscuits?

ARNOLD. You left out the best part.

TRUDY. Yes, yes, of course, my love. You may have your plate of Dried Spam Bites. Anything for my new friend Arnold.

> *(***ARNOLD** *nods. He also smiles.* **CHARLIE** *ends his call and returns to the others, his expression fixed and grim.)*

TRUDY. What's wrong? Is Barbara ill?

CHARLIE. No. Mama's fine. She's really excited about the money. She still can't believe you're doing this.

PATTY. Then what is it? What's the matter, Charlie?

MAYVONNE. *(To CHARLIE.)* What did she say to you, honey?

CHARLIE. Oh. Okay.

(Slowly, trying to get it right.) She's very happy about the money – especially about not having to wait until Ms. Tromaine dies to get it. And then she started thinking about what she'd like to do with it.

VALERIE. You mean *do* with her two million.

CHARLIE. No. I mean do with her *sixteen* million.

PATTY. Charlie, did you really hear that right?

(**CHARLIE** *nods.*)

CORINNE. Barbara doesn't plan to share *any* of that money with us?

(**CHARLIE** *shakes his head.*)

MAMIE. *(Exploding.)* I KNEW IT! I KNEW IT! I KNEW IT!

MAYVONNE. Oh no, this isn't good.

(**MAYVONNE** *sits down. She, like the others, is stunned.* **FLOSSIE** *throws an arm around* **MAMIE** *to try to calm her down.*)

MAMIE. *(To CHARLIE.)* What else did your mother say? Let's have the rest of it.

CHARLIE. *(Uneasily.)* She said that after all these years of having to put up with all of you and all your idiosyncrasies and all your varying degrees of maddening behavior, that she was finally getting properly compensated. And she told me to thank everyone for the money and to tell all of you that she has a lot more respect for each of you now for having the good sense to award it to the person who knows best how to use it.

(Beat.)

And she's thinking about buying a yacht.

(*A short, deadly silence.*)

VALERIE. (*To* **TRUDY**.) So after all you put us through, we get to watch Barbara Seaburn, who didn't have to put up with *any* of this, sail blissfully off into the sunset in her *yacht*?

TRUDY. Well, Valerie, you all know that Charlie was just here as her proxy. Barbara's the Glitter Girl. She wears the tiara. And as I explained: the winner of the game has every right to decide what she'd like to do with her winnings.

(*Others sit down, hardly able, now, to speak.*)

ARNOLD. Anybody want a drink?

MAMIE. Do you have any hemlock?

CORINNE. (*To* **CHARLIE**.) You don't happen to have your mother's tiara, do you?

CHARLIE. Actually, I do.

CORINNE. I'd like to look at it, if you don't mind.

CHARLIE. I don't mind. Just so long as I don't have to put it on.

(*He gets up and heads toward the porch, where he'll pull a tiara from the bag he brought with him.*)

FLOSSIE. (*To* **CORINNE**.) Now honey, why do you need to see Barbara Seaburn's tiara? Weren't all of our tiaras made at the same time by that there New York jeweler friend of Trudy's?

TRUDY. You have a very good memory, Flossie, ol' girl.

PATTY. And those tiaras represent something very special – a symbol of our bond and our friendship. My mother always told me this. And I remember that you all had to talk me out of having Mama buried with hers. You all know how much it meant to her.

MAYVONNE. (*Touching with affection the tiara* **PATTY** *wears.*) I'm so glad you kept it for yourself, Patty. Because it really becomes you.

PATTY. Thank you, Mayvonne.

> (**CHARLIE** *returns to the group with his mother's tiara in hand.* **CORINNE** *approaches and takes it from him. She gives it a close inspection.*)

CORINNE. As I thought.

FLOSSIE. What?

CORINNE. *(To* **CHARLIE.***)* This isn't a Glitter Girl tiara. This is just some costume-jewelry thing she probably ordered online.

TRUDY. *(To* **CORINNE.***)* How can you tell?

CORINNE. Well, for one thing: look at it. It doesn't look anything at all like ours. Second: I happen to know something about her original tiara, because of something that happened that day Dabney and I went to her law office about the DUI. We got to fussing over why she didn't want to take his case and first thing you know, Barbara is saying that being a Glitter Girl has been nothing but trouble for her from the very beginning. And she doesn't think she even wants to be one anymore, and then she yanks open one of her desk drawers and takes out that expensive tiara that Trudy got her and flings it against the wall. It broke into so many pieces I guess she couldn't get it repaired.

MAYVONNE. When did this happen, Corinne?

CORINNE. About three years ago, I think.

FLOSSIE. And we never noticed, in our last three years of meetings, that Barbara was wearin' a goddang *fake* tiara?

MAMIE. We can be terribly unobservant, can't we?

VALERIE. *(Examining the fake tiara.)* No, I hadn't noticed it either.

TRUDY. I'm trying to process what Corinne just said. I'm trying to process how Babs could have had so much contempt for all of us.

VALERIE. Excuse me, Trudy, but you yourself said we were a disappointment. You set up this whole thing to find out just how undeserving we were when it came to any of us getting your money.

TRUDY. That's right. And I happened to find out some things this afternoon that didn't make me very happy. In fact, I think I can honestly say I've never met a more *dysfunctional* group of people in all my life. But after hearing about all your struggles and listening to those stories of courage *and* out-right idiocy, and even though you snipped and sniped and tried at times to pull the rug out from under each other – and let's face it, Valerie – you *are* a whore, but Mamie: your husband's a politician, and, honey, there ain't a dime's worth of difference between those two in *my* book – even after all that, I can safely say there isn't another bunch of women on this entire planet who I could love more – in spite of your faults. So no, I will not be giving this money to Barbara Seaburn to buy a yacht for herself – Barbara Seaburn, who forfeited her right to be a Glitter Girl when she shattered her Gleam-and-Sparkle against a wall. I give it to Charlie, the daughter she never had. I move that as of this day we make Charlie a Glitter Girl. Not just an *honorary* Glitter Girl like Dowd, but a G.G. in full. Do I hear a second?

PATTY. *(Excitedly.)* I second!

TRUDY. All in favor?

  (All the women raise their hands.)

And if my fellow ladies of the Shimmer and Shine agree, Charlie, I will allow you to claim that money not as your mother's proxy but for yourself, to do with as *you* choose.

CHARLIE. *(Stunned.)* Wow.

  (Pulling himself together.)

Thank you, Ms. Tromaine.

  (Turning to the others.)

CHARLIE. I won't disappoint you.

TRUDY. I might suggest, though, that you withhold at least one dollar from Ms. Flossie Price here, for saying all those mean things about my family and my birth holler.

FLOSSIE. I can live with that.

(*Beat, then warmly:*)

And: I'm sorry.

(**PATTY** *is so moved by what* **TRUDY** *has just said and done that she throws her arms around* **TRUDY***'s neck and gives her a big kiss.*)

MAYVONNE. Though what you did to us, Trudy, does come close to being unforgivable.

TRUDY. Well, you'll all have years and years of living the high life to find it in your hearts to forgive me.

(**MAYVONNE** *nods and smiles.*)

CORINNE. (*To* **TRUDY.**) And you're really serious – I mean about not making us wait until you're dead to get that money?

TRUDY. (*To* **CORINNE.**) Making you all wait: now *that* would be unforgivable. We Tromaines have the long-genes. Members of my family have been known to live well into their nineties.

CHARLIE. (*Worried.*) My mother's going to have a cow when she finds out what just happened.

TRUDY. I'm perfectly fine with that. You also need to tell Barbara that I've decided to take all my legal business to a different law firm, and once you start your own practice, Charlie, I just might send a little of it *your* way.

CHARLIE. (*Brightening.*) I think I'd like that.

(**PATTY** *is now staring at the back of* **CHARLIE***'s neck. She traces the "swirls" with her finger. His smile of contentment switches to a frown, though, when* **CORINNE** *plops the tiara on his head.*)

TRUDY. *(Tickled, as are the other Glitter Girls.)* You wear it *so* nicely!

> *(Turning to* **ARPEGE.***)*

How about my butler goes and makes me one of those gin rickeys everybody's been lapping up around here.

ARNOLD. *(With a straight face.)* Coming right up, ma'am.

> *(As he passes* **TRUDY** *he kisses her sweetly on the forehead. She beams.)*

DOWD. I was wondering if you could all do me a favor.

TRUDY. *(To* **DOWD.***)* What's that?

DOWD. Mary Katherine said there was this song you always sang at the end of your meetings. I've always wondered about it.

TRUDY. *(To her fellow Glitter Girls.)* Shall we, ladies?

> *(Nods all around. The G.G.s all join hands and sing their anthem to the tune "Glow Worm."* The lights do a slow fade-out.**)*

THE GLITTER GIRLS.

> SHINE LITTLE GLITTER GIRL, GLIMMER, GLIMMER.
> SHINE LITTLE GLITTER GIRL, GLIMMER, GLIMMER.
> ALL JOIN HANDS AND TREK AND WANDER.
> FRIENDS AND SISTERS NEAR AND YONDER.
> SHINE LITTLE GLITTER GIRL, GLIMMER, GLIMMER.
> HEY THERE, DON'T GET DIMMER, DIMMER.
> LIGHT THE PATH ABOVE, BELOW,
> AND SPARKLE AS WE GO!

End of Play

---

*Licensees should use Paul Lincke's 1902 version of the "Glow Worm" melody.

**Note: An alternate staging of this final moment could include bringing the women downstage to sing their song directly to the audience. By inviting the three men to join them, set-up for a ready-made curtain call could easily be effected.